Saved by a Saint

Also by Barbara Cartland in Large Print:

The Eyes of Love

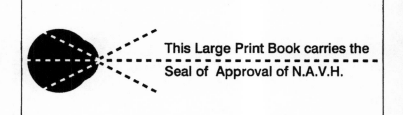

This Large Print Book carries the Seal of Approval of N.A.V.H.

Saved by a Saint

Barbara Cartland

Thorndike Press • Thorndike, Maine

Published in 1996 by arrangement with
The Berkley Publishing Group.

Thorndike Large Print® Romance Series.

The tree indicium is a trademark of Thorndike Press.

The text of this Large Print edition is unabridged.
Other aspects of the book may vary from the original edition.

Set in 16 pt. Bookman Old Style by Al Chase.

Printed in the United States on permanent paper.

Library of Congress Cataloging in Publication Data

Cartland, Barbara, 1902–
    Saved by a saint / Barbara Cartland.
    p.   cm.
    ISBN 0-7862-0646-2 (lg. print : hc)
    1. Large type books. I. Title.
    [PR6005.A765S28 1996]
    823'.912—dc20   95-52454

Author's Note

Like a great number of other people, I always have a medallion of St. Christopher in my car. I believe it keeps me safe from accidents, and I would not be without it.

Christopher, who was born around the third century, is the Patron Saint of Travellers. He was martyred under the Emperor Decius about A.D. 250.

He has always been the hero of many legends, which represent him as a giant who, after being converted to Christianity, dedicated his life to carrying travellers on his back across a river.

One day when he was at work, a very small child asked to be taken across.

In the middle of the river the child became so heavy that Christopher staggered under the weight of him.

"If I had borne the whole world on my back," he said, "it could not have weighed heavier than you."

"That is not surprising," the child replied, "for you have borne upon your back the world, and He who created it."

That is the reason why the St. Christopher medallion usually depicts him carrying the Christ Child on his back.

His Feast Day is 25th July in the Western Church, and 9th May in the Orthodox Church.

chapter one

1819

The Marquis of Melverley left London in a bad temper.

He had not intended to go to the country, but then he had seen Lady Bray.

There had been an uncomfortable altercation which had left the Marquis seething with rage.

Lady Bray was one of the most famous Beauties of the year and the toast of St. James's.

She had bestowed her favours on quite a number of men before she met the Marquis.

He, however, swept her off her feet and their *affaire de coeur* was the talk of the *Beau Monde.*

Everything was going smoothly, until Lord Bray returned from the country.

It was then he told his wife that he was taking her away from London.

Lady Bray was horrified.

She was at the height of her success.

She was asked to every party and was convinced in her own mind that the

Prince Regent could not give a successful dinner at Carlton House unless she
was present.

She pleaded with her husband, but
he was adamant.

"You are being talked about," he said.
"I will not have my good name dragged
through the mud!"

When Daisy Bray broke the news to
the Marquis, he was astonished.

It was more or less accepted that,
when a man had been married for some
years and his wife had produced an heir
to the title, he closed his eyes if she
indulged in flirtations, or something
deeper, with other men.

Lord Bray was, however, a very proud
man.

When one of his sisters told him what
was being said in Mayfair, he came to
London.

"Nothing I can say will alter his decision that we leave for the country on
Friday," Daisy said tearfully to the Marquis.

"But I cannot lose you," he protested.
"How can you possibly give up all the
parties and Balls you have promised to
attend — and of course — me!"

"I mind that more than anything,"

Daisy said in a soft voice, putting a hand on his arm, "but it is no use. When Arthur makes up his mind, as he has now, I have to obey him."

Lord Bray's decision upset the Marquis.

But he had gone for consolation to the house in Chelsea where he had established his mistress.

She was one of the loveliest Ballerinas, appearing at Drury Lane.

Letty Lesse was an exceptional dancer and exceptional in anything else she undertook.

This included capturing the hearts of the innumerable men who pursued her.

She was, however, thrilled when the Marquis turned his attention to her.

She was well aware that he was more important and certainly richer than any of her other suitors.

She accepted with alacrity that she should move from the lodgings where she was living into the attractive house in Chelsea.

It had been occupied by one person before her.

The Marquis was, however, quite weary of the quest because of her tiresome habit of giggling at whatever he said.

She also bit her nails.

It was considered fashionable for the Bucks and *Beaux* of St. James's to have a "Cyprian" who was exclusively their own.

That was, of course, if they could afford it.

No one could afford it better than the Marquis of Melverley.

He had inherited an enormous Estate when he was twenty-six.

It had been in his family for three hundred years, and had been added to by every generation.

His Father had been the third Marquis and he was the fourth.

He was extremely proud of his title, his blood, and his position in life.

Although he was only twenty-eight, the Prince Regent had told him he was to be Lord Lieutenant of the County as soon as the appointment was available.

His Royal Highness had also indicated that there would be a position for him at Court as soon as he became King.

The Marquis accepted all this as his due.

He had shone dramatically in Wellington's Army and received two awards for bravery.

He was well aware that although he was so young, Statesmen listened to what he had to say.

The Prince Regent, too, consulted him on a number of the problems which beset him every day.

He had left Daisy Bray in tears at the idea that she would have to leave London without seeing him alone again.

He thought he would try to forget her attractions in the arms of Letty Lesse.

The Marquis had neglected Letty over the last three weeks.

Because Lord Bray was in the country, he had spent every evening, and most of the night, with Daisy.

He was thinking now how attractive Letty was when she danced.

She knew how to make a man forget his troubles when she put her arms around his neck.

He had to go first to a dinner that was taking place at the Duke of Bedford's house in Islington.

He was feeling depressed, and it did nothing to revive his spirits.

Actually he decided that the ladies sitting on each side of him at dinner were bores.

None of those present compared in

any way with Daisy or with Letty.

The dinner dragged on until finally it came to an end.

Afterwards there was music and card-games at which he was obliged to participate.

It was nearly midnight when he finally climbed into his carriage.

It was drawn by two superb horses and he told his coachman to take him to Chelsea.

There was a faint grin, which he did not see, on his Coachman's face.

The footman gave the Coachman a wink as they drove off.

"It's like ol' times," the latter murmured beneath his breath. "Them 'orses used to know their own way there."

The Coachman chuckled.

But what he was thinking was that it was going to be a long night.

He knew his wife would complain bitterly when he woke her up just before dawn.

It was not far to the Marquis's house in Chelsea, which was near the famous Hospital inaugurated by Nell Gwynn.

In front of it was a Square where trees had been planted.

The Coachman drew the horses up with a flourish outside the front-door.

The Marquis got out.

It was understood that the footman did not ring for the maid he employed.

By this time she would have gone to bed.

The Marquis had his own latch-key with which to open the door.

Inserting it in the lock, he was thinking that at this hour Letty would have come back from the Theatre.

She would be in bed, but would be delighted to see him, especially as he had neglected her for so long.

She would hold out her arms and be far too clever to reproach him in any way.

He opened the door.

As he expected, there was a light in the hall from candles in two silver sconces.

He had brought them up from his house in the country.

He had given orders that they were always to be left alight.

If he arrived unexpectedly, he had no wish to fumble in the dark.

He shut the front-door behind him and put the key in his pocket.

He took off his tall hat.

He was about to put it on the chair, where he usually left it.

It was then he saw there was another hat already there.

It was the same shape and, in fact, almost identical.

He stared at it in surprise.

He wondered when he had left it there and gone home without it.

Suddenly he was suspicious.

He put his own hat down on a table in front of a gold-framed mirror.

This had also come from his house in the country.

Deliberately quiet, he went up the thickly carpeted stairs.

There was a small landing with a door on either side of it.

One led into a small room that was seldom used.

The other room was much larger and was where Letty slept.

The Marquis had gone to a lot of trouble to furnish it to his own taste.

The extra-large bed had a golden co-rolla above it from which fell curtains that were of the finest silk.

He had excellent taste.

He hated the harsh colours and taw-

14

dry decorations that were to be found in most Cyprians' bedrooms.

If he was going to keep a mistress, then he was determined that her background should be to his taste, and not hers.

Very soft colours decorated Letty's bedroom.

The expensive materials used were the envy and admiration of the other girls who danced with her.

The carpet was a fine Aubusson.

The pictures on the walls were by French artists.

The furniture had come, like much of the Prince Regent's, from the Palace at Versailles after the Revolution.

As the Marquis reached the landing, he stood still for a moment before he reached for the handle.

It was then, as he heard Letty laughing, that he was frozen into immobility.

For a moment he did not believe his ears.

Then, as the laugh was followed by a man's deep voice, he realised that Letty was betraying him.

It was an unwritten law that, when a Cyprian was housed and kept by a Protector, she was faithful to him for as

15

long as he was generous to her.

The Marquis had certainly been that.

Letty's diamonds and pearls were sensational.

He had somewhat neglected her these past weeks.

Yet, it had never struck him for a moment that she would take another lover.

And certainly not in *his* house without first ending their association.

The fact that she had done so made him very angry.

He contemplated for a moment walking into the bedroom and telling her exactly what he thought of her.

Then he knew it was beneath his dignity to do so.

When the Marquis was angry, he never raised his voice or ranted at anyone.

Instead, he became icily calm and merely spoke in a voice in which every word cut like a whiplash.

Now he turned and walked down the stairs.

Picking up his hat, he stood for a moment looking at his reflection in the gold-framed mirror.

Then, deliberately, one by one, he

16

blew out the four candles that lit the hall.

He wondered if it would alert Letty to the fact that he had been there.

At any rate, to-morrow morning she would receive a note from his Secretary, telling her to vacate the premises.

Then there would be no doubt in her mind what had happened.

Having put out the candles, he went out of the house, closing the door quietly behind him.

The Coachman and footman had settled themselves as comfortably as they could on the box, expecting a long wait.

They therefore stared in astonishment when the Marquis returned so soon.

The footman sprang down and opened the carriage door.

"Take me home!" the Marquis said quietly.

"Very good, M'Lord," the Coachman replied. The door was shut and the carriage started off.

As it did so, the Marquis decided that he would go to the country.

He had no wish to see Daisy again, looking at him unhappily while her husband glared.

And he had finished completely and absolutely with Letty.

He had a sudden longing for the quiet and beauty of Melverley Hall.

He would ride his horses over the Estate knowing that it was his and his alone.

No-one could take it from him.

When he reached his house in Berkeley Square, he gave several sharp orders to the Night-Footman.

He then went upstairs to his bedroom, where his Valet was waiting for him.

The Marquis had learned during the war to sleep deeply and completely when he had the chance.

He could wake at whatever time he chose.

Nevertheless, he told his Valet to call him at seven-thirty.

He also ordered his Travelling Phaeton should be brought round at nine o'clock.

"I am going to the country, Yates," he said. "Follow me in the Brake with the luggage and tell the Head Chef he is to come with us."

"Very good, M'Lord," Yates answered.

He showed no surprise that the Marquis was leaving so unexpectedly.

He had been with him, fighting in Portugal and with the Army of Occupation in France.

He was always prepared for any emergency without making a fuss.

The Marquis, having finished his breakfast, sent for his Secretary.

He gave him instructions that Letty Lesse was to leave his house in Chelsea immediately.

His Secretary, Mr. Barlow, who had been with him for some years, made no comment.

He was, however, more concerned when the Marquis told him to cancel all his arrangements for the next week.

"All, My Lord?" he expostulated. "But the party on Tuesday night is being given especially in Your Lordship's honour. And His Royal Highness is expecting you to drive with him on Thursday to Wimbledon to watch a Mill."

"Make what excuses you like," the Marquis said. "Say I have to bury a relative, or take part in a Christening, but I am definitely leaving London!"

Mr. Barlow sighed.

But he merely said, in the same way

that the other servants in the house took their orders:

"Very good, my Lord."

The Marquis set off, driving a new team of horses.

Later his anger began to subside a little.

It was not so much that he was re-gretting losing Daisy.

It was that he loathed above all things being made to look a fool.

That was exactly what Letty had done to him.

He thought of the presents he had given her and the trouble he had taken to re-decorate the house.

He had made it a perfect background for her unusual beauty.

He thought, too, that whoever had taken his place in bed last night would also be laughing up his sleeve.

He had no wish to know who it was. That was immaterial.

What he disliked was that, having trusted a woman, she had proved un-trustworthy.

The Marquis was not particularly con-ceited, considering how much he had to be conceited about.

But he would have been a fool if he

had not been aware that he had an enormous attraction for women.

Where a Cyprian was concerned, it was not only what he gave her that counted in their affair, they invariably fell in love with him as well.

Part of the arrangement was that there would be no recriminations and no reproaches when an affair of that sort came to an end.

But where he was concerned, there were invariably tears and reproaches, also the inevitable questions.

"What have I done? Why do you not love me any more?"

It was not, as he knew only too well, a question of love.

Yet a woman like Letty, who could attract a great number of men and to whom they meant nothing of any consequence, would inevitably give him her heart.

He had grown used to this unusual occurrence.

That Letty had betrayed him, however, came as a shock.

It was certainly something he had never experienced before, neither with the Lettys of this world, nor with Ladies like Daisy.

21

He had admitted to himself often enough that they had little to talk about when he was not making love to them.

He could not help feeling that it was entirely Daisy's fault that her husband had turned nasty.

The Marquis was always very particular not to betray his feelings in public.

People talked, whoever he was with.

It was impossible to keep an *affaire de coeur* a complete secret.

But Daisy, in her joy at having captured his affection, had been very obvious.

The unrestrained passion in her eyes, her lips, and every movement of her body was apparent to the gossips.

The whole of the *Beau Monde* was soon talking about them.

It was therefore to be expected that sooner or later Lord Bray would be informed.

The Marquis had to admit that in the circumstances there was nothing else Lord Bray could do but take his wife away from London.

This, as the Marquis knew, would cause a further outbreak of chatter.

It would undoubtedly reverberate throughout Mayfair.

He thought of how his friends, and

especially his enemies, would chuckle at his discomfiture.

Lord Bray had not challenged him to a duel, which would have been damaging to Daisy's reputation.

He was, instead, taking her to the country.

In their home she was for the moment out of danger.

"Dammit all!" the Marquis swore. "I have been made to look a fool, not only by Letty Lesse, but also by Arthur Bray."

He drove his horses with his usual expertise, fast but in no way pushing them.

The sunshine glittered on their harness and shone on the road ahead.

The Marquis knew he should have been enjoying himself.

The groom sitting beside him was aware that his Master's lips were set in a hard line.

There was also a frightening expression in his eyes.

It made everyone who worked for him feel when they saw it as if a trickle of icy water were moving down their backs.

The Marquis drove on.

He stopped after two hours to change horses at a Posting-Inn, where another team belonging to him was waiting.

While the animals were being changed over, he drank a glass of home-made cider.

He refused the wine the Inn-keeper offered him.

He was, in fact, always abstemious both in what he ate and what he drank.

As they started out again, he was thinking of the horses that would be waiting for him in the stables at the Hall.

He expected to be there within an hour-and-a-half.

His Secretary had sent a groom across country to alert the servants of his imminent arrival.

It was nearly one o'clock when the Marquis turned his carriage round a corner on the Highway, then pulled them up sharply.

Just ahead there had been a collision, and a bad one.

A large, overloaded coach could only just have fallen sideways on the road.

The panic-stricken horses which had been pulling it were struggling wildly against the sharp shafts.

There was a country wagon with a shattered wheel on the other side of the road.

Somehow mixed up in the middle of it all was a pony-cart, and the animal that had been pulling it was lying on the ground.

There were screams and shouts coming from the occupants of the coach, and the whole scene was one of chaos.

The Marquis handed his reins to the groom and jumped down to the ground.

Then he started to create order out of the chaos.

He ordered some labourers, who had appeared, to help free the horses belonging to the coach.

Two other men were told to release the shafts of the carthorse drawing the farm wagon.

He then assisted those inside the coach who were either screaming or in tears to clamber with some difficulty onto the road.

One woman seemed rather badly crushed by those who had fallen against her when the carriage toppled over.

The Marquis told some boys who were watching with interest to go and find the nearest Doctor.

The biggest of the boys, who seemed older than the others, told the Marquis he knew where he lived.

The Marquis gave the boy a shilling and told him to run as fast as he could.

Delighted with the generous tip, the boy set off and the Marquis looked round him.

The men and women he had helped from the coach were standing disconsolately by the roadside.

They were making no effort to retrieve their luggage which had been thrown over the roof of the coach and was in the ditch.

Some of the lids had come off the boxes and the contents were strewn over the grass and the road.

The Marquis told them to retrieve their belongings.

He then looked at the pony cart.

Beside it a girl knelt, stroking the pony's neck. It was lying still.

As he reached her, the girl looked up at him and he saw that she was very pretty.

"I . . . I . . . my p-pony . . . is . . . d-dead," she said in a broken little voice.

26

The Marquis bent down and saw immediately that she was right.

It was a very old pony.

A wheel had been broken by the coach as it crashed against the wagon.

It had hit the animal with enough violence to kill it.

Undoubtedly, the Marquis thought, the pony would not have lived long anyway.

But to the girl stroking it with long, thin fingers, it was a tragedy.

"I am sorry," he said quietly, "but I am afraid there is nothing that can be done."

"D-do you think that . . . perhaps I could . . . have him . . . b-buried?" she asked.

"I am sure that can be managed," the Marquis replied.

He saw a labourer standing watching the horses belonging to the coach.

They were now more or less under control.

"There is a dead pony here," the Marquis said to him, "and the owner wants him buried. Have you any suggestions about where this can be done?"

The labourer realised he was being spoken to by someone in authority, and he touched his forelock.

"Oi'll do it fer ye," he said, "if that be what's wanted."

"That is what I want," the Marquis agreed. "I will pay you for doing so."

He walked back to the girl, and the labourer followed him.

The Marquis gave the orders because he saw that the girl was fighting back her tears.

When the labourer took the sovereign he was offered, his eyes gleamed.

He offered to find a friend of his who would help him with the task.

"There be a bit o' wasteland, Sor," he said, "jes' as ye comes into t'village. We'll put 'im there."

"Thank you . . . thank you . . . very much," the girl said in a breathless little voice. "I . . . I will . . . come back . . . to-morrow . . . and see where you have . . . buried . . . him."

"That's right, Miss," the labourer said, "an' don' 'e worry. If ye wants to put up a tombstone to 'e, Oi'll do that wi' some wood."

"That is very . . . kind of . . . you," the girl said. "He was called . . . Ben and . . . I have had him . . . ever since I was . . . little."

"Then Oi knows as 'ow ye'll miss 'e," the labourer said.

She nodded, and the Marquis said:

"I think I had better take you home. If I can find someone to repair your cart, you will be able to fetch it later."

"Oi'll de that fer ye, Sor," the labourer said eagerly.

"That would be very helpful," the Marquis said.

As another sovereign exchanged hands, he knew the man would keep his word.

Then he turned to the girl and said:

"Now let me take you home. We can do nothing more here."

She went with him to his Phaeton, and the Marquis helped her into it.

The groom who had been holding the horses' heads jumped up onto the seat behind.

It was not easy for the Marquis to negotiate his way past the upturned coach.

The wagon had now been pushed to one side, the horse having been released.

Somehow the Marquis managed it and the road ahead was clear.

As he drove on, he asked:

"What is your name?"

"I am . . . Christina Churston," she replied.

The Marquis thought for a moment. Then he said:

"I think you live on my Estate."

"Yes . . . I do," she agreed, "and I know you are the . . . Marquis of Melverley."

The Marquis smiled and turned to look at her.

She was, he told himself, exceptionally lovely, but she was simply dressed.

It was then he noticed that she was wearing a black sash round the waist of her white gown.

"I have been abroad during the war," he said, "and since I returned, I do not think I have met your family."

"My . . . my Father d-died a fortnight ago," Christina answered. "I live at . . . Four Gables . . . just outside your Park."

"Of course, I remember now hearing of your Father," the Marquis remarked. "Did he not have a large stamp collection?"

"Yes, that is right," Christina said. "He collected stamps all his life, and as your Father also had a collection, they used to meet and compare notes."

"I remember my Father telling me about that," the Marquis said. "I am very sorry to hear that he is no longer with you."

"I . . . miss him . . . very much," Christina said.

There was a forlorn note in her voice which made the Marquis ask:

"Are you telling me that you are living alone at Four Gables?"

"I . . . I have my Nanny . . . with me," Christina replied, "and I have . . . written to Papa's brother . . . but his family live in Northumberland . . . and it is a very . . . very long way . . . away."

"It is indeed," the Marquis agreed, "but I do not think you ought to be alone."

"I . . . I am not alone," Christina said, "but I shall miss . . . B-Ben. It was the one way I could go and visit my friends . . . and now I shall have to walk."

She spoke so naturally that the Marquis knew she was not asking him to be generous and provide her with some other form of transport.

By now they had turned into the village.

There was a row of thatched cottages on one side of the road and on the other the wall surrounding the Marquis's Estate.

He drove past his own gates.

He remembered that further up the road there was a charming red brick Elizabethan house.

He had thought when he was small that it had a funny name.

He could not, however, remember ever having met Christina.

"How old are you," he asked, "if that is not a rude question?"

"I am eighteen," Christina answered. "I will be nineteen in three months time."

That explained, the Marquis thought, why he had not seen her.

He had gone off to war as soon as he had left Eton.

He had thought in those days that young girls were a bore and beneath his dignity.

He steered his horses down the short drive, then pulled up outside the front-door of Four Gables.

"I am going to leave you now," he said, "but I will come and call on you some time tomorrow and see if I can help you over the loss of your pony."

"That is . . . very kind of you," Christina said, "but you must not . . . bother yourself . . . when you have . . .

so many . . . other things to see to."

The Marquis raised his eye-brows, and she added:

"The whole village has been longing for you to come home. They need your guidance on so many things that have to be done which, of course, were neglected while you were in France."

"Neglected?" the Marquis repeated in surprise.

It had never occurred to him that while he was away, things were not being carried on exactly as they were in his Father's time.

"The war has made a great difference," Christina said as if he had asked the question. "Now the men are coming back from the Army and they are looking for work."

"They will be employed, as they always have been, on the Estate," the Marquis said sharply.

She did not speak, and he looked at her.

"What are you trying to tell me?" he asked.

"I . . . I am . . . sorry . . . it is not . . . my business," Christina replied.

She got out of the Phaeton as she spoke.

The Marquis followed her as his groom went to the horses' heads.

Christina opened the front-door and he walked after her into the small hall.

"I want you to explain what you have been saying," he said. "Is there trouble here that I do not know about?"

She looked at him uncertainly.

"I ought . . . not to . . . interfere," she said, "and I . . . I spoke without . . . thinking."

"But I want you to think," the Marquis said. "I want you to tell me the truth. What is wrong?"

"I think you should talk to the Vicar," Christina said. "He is very worried, as Papa was, about the young men having . . . nothing to do."

"I will certainly see to it," the Marquis said. "Thank you for telling me. I will come and see you to-morrow."

"Thank you for being . . . so kind about . . . Ben. I know you gave that man . . . quite a lot of money . . . and of course I must . . . pay you . . . back," replied Christina.

"I should be insulted if you did anything of the sort!" the Marquis said as he smiled.

"Then . . . thank you . . . thank you

very much," Christina said again.

The Marquis got back into his Phaeton, turned it round, and raising his hat drove back up the drive.

He was thinking as he went that something was unmistakably wrong.

It was fortunate that he had found out about it, even though it was in such an unexpected manner.

And yet the mere idea of there being anything wrong at Melverley annoyed him.

"I wonder what the devil it is!" he asked himself as he drove in at his lodge gates.

chapter two

The Butler was waiting in the hall when the Marquis arrived.

With him were four footmen whose livery seemed somewhat ill-fitting.

"Welcome back, M'Lord!" the Butler said. "It's good to have Your Lordship back."

"I should have come earlier," the Marquis replied, "but I was kept in London. However, I agree with you, Johnson, it is a joy to be back."

He looked around the large hall.

With the sun shining on the gold frames of his ancestors' portraits, he thought it looked very impressive.

"Luncheon's ready, M'Lord," Johnson said.

The Marquis, however, walked towards the room which was at the far end of the Hall.

It was where his Mother had always sat and where he had last seen his Father.

The Third Marquis had died while his son was fighting in Portugal and he had been unable to return for the Funeral.

Here again everything seemed exactly

as it had been when he was a child —
the books with their leather covers on
the shelves, the pieces of furniture
which were very old and had been
handed down through the generations.

The Marquis without any comment
turned round and walked down the
corridor to the Dining-Room.

This was a magnificent room which
could comfortably seat a hundred
people without it seeming over-
crowded.

The Minstrels' Gallery at the far end,
with its carved front, had been a delight
when he was a small boy.

He remembered how he had crept
downstairs when his Father and Mother
were giving a party.

He would peep at them without being
seen.

He recalled how radiantly beautiful
his Mother had looked wearing the
Melverley tiara.

Round her neck were rows of pearls
that reached almost to her knees.

He decided that one day he would give
the same sort of parties.

But he doubted if anyone, not even
those as beautiful as Daisy, would compare with his Mother.

The food which he was served was excellent.

Mr. Barlow had been wise enough to warn the cook at the Hall that His Lordship preferred small meals.

As soon as he had finished, the Marquis said:

"I now wish to see Mr. Waters. I suppose he is in the Estate Office?"

Johnson hesitated, and the Marquis waited.

"I — I don't think Mr. Waters is here yet, M'Lord," he said after what seemed a considerable pause.

"Not here?" the Marquis exclaimed. "Why not? Where is he?"

"Mr. Waters usually comes in during the afternoons, M'Lord," Johnson replied.

"He did not know that I was arriving to-day?"

"No, M'Lord. We didn't expect Your Lordship so early, so there was no reason to notify him."

The Marquis thought the explanation was rather strange.

There was also an expression on Johnson's face that confirmed his conviction that all was not well.

Without saying any more, he walked out of the Dining-Room and down a long corridor which led to the Estate Office.

It was at the far end of the house, and as he remembered, was a large room.

The walls were decorated with maps of the Estate, and black despatch boxes were piled up in one corner.

As the Marquis expected, there was no-one there, and the room seemed untidy.

The large desk at which Waters worked was piled high with account books, one of them open.

The Marquis glanced at it.

Then he saw that his Estate Manager had been working on the accounts for the month.

While he was in France, the Estate had been left in Waters's hands.

He sent an account every month to his Solicitors in London to obtain the wages.

It was an arrangement the Marquis had made before his Father's death.

He had thought it was too much for him to cope with the day-to-day difficulties of the Estate when he was in ill health.

He looked at the book now, then began to turn over the pages one by one.

Christina Churston had said that the young men of the village as well as those returning from the war were unemployed.

It was something he could not understand.

When his Father was alive, everybody in the village was employed in one way or another at what they called the "Big House."

The best-looking young men started as Pantry Boys and rose to be footmen.

Others worked in the garden or became grooms, Game-Keepers, Carpenters, Bricklayers, or Blacksmiths.

If they were fond of animals, they were found a place at the Home Farm.

Melverley was a State within a State.

It was something that had continued all down the centuries.

It was unheard of, unless there was something wrong with them, for the young women not to be employed at the Big House.

The Marquis went down the list of names carefully.

Then he stiffened as he read: "*Jim Hicks.*"

He remembered Jim Hicks well. He

had taught him to ride when he had his first pony.

Jim had been badly wounded at Waterloo and the Marquis had gone to find him after the battle.

He had been taken to a ruined Church which had lost its roof and one of its walls due to cannon fire.

There was, however, some shelter left.

The wounded had been set down on the stone floor as they were carried from the battlefield.

It had taken the Marquis a little time to find Jim.

When he did, he saw he had been shot in the chest and had lost a leg.

There was obviously no chance of him surviving.

As the Marquis knelt down beside him, he said:

"I am sorry to see you like this, Jim."

With an effort, the man managed to croak:

"Us won, didn't us, M'Lord!"

"We won!" the Marquis confirmed. "You did splendidly and it was a great victory!"

Jim had smiled.

Then he had closed his eyes and the

Marquis knew he would not open them again.

He could remember all too well what he had felt as he left the Church.

Jim, who had been a part of his childhood, had gone for ever.

Now he looked again at Waters's accounts.

Turning back a few pages, he saw that Jim's wages had been entered every month since the Battle of Waterloo, a battle that had taken place nearly four years ago!

The Marquis had a very astute brain and he knew precisely how Waters had been "cooking the books."

Here was the reason why the men returning from the Army and Navy were unemployed.

Alive or dead, Waters was drawing their wages and putting the money into his own pocket.

The mere idea of how so many had been deprived made the Marquis furiously angry.

At the same time, he stiffened and his mouth was set in a hard line.

He went back to the Study and rang the bell for Johnson.

"As soon as Mr. Waters comes in," he

said, "send him to me here."

"Very good, M'Lord."

The Marquis hesitated for a moment. Then he asked:

"How long have you been working at the Hall, Johnson?"

"Since I were twelve, M'Lord," Johnson replied. "That be nigh on thirty-seven years."

"And you never thought to tell me what was going on?" the Marquis asked.

Johnson did not pretend to misunderstand.

"Your Lordship were a-fighting abroad, and I didn't want t' worry you."

What he was implying, the Marquis realised, was that he might easily have been killed, in which case, he could have done nothing about it.

Then Waters would undoubtedly have had Johnson dismissed.

The Marquis did not speak, and after a moment Johnson said:

"I'm sorry, M'Lord, an' we're all a-praying that things'll get back to being as they used to be."

"They will!" the Marquis answered. "But I wish I had known about this sooner."

He had to admit to himself that it was partly his fault.

Wellington had kept him in the Army of Occupation for far longer than he had expected.

He knew, of course, that he was being useful to the General by staying in France.

He had not only coped with the troops.

Diplomats were coming to Paris from every country in the world.

There were a great number of decisions to be made, and much to discuss.

There was also, undoubtedly, for a young man who had spent the years since he had left School fighting, the thrill of being in Paris.

Anything the French could do to alleviate their Conquerors' trials and tribulations was done.

They did it with an expertise and charm that was irresistible.

It was typical of the French that they tried to turn what had been a defeat into a victory.

As far as the Diplomats and those in the Army of Occupation were concerned, they succeeded.

Now the Marquis was thinking that as soon as he returned to England, he should have come to Melverley immediately.

44

The War Office, however, had required his presence almost daily.

The Prince Regent had shown him a friendliness that was the envy of all his contemporaries.

He was always included in the invitations to dine at Carlton House.

Because he had been in France, the Prince Regent consulted him about pictures, furniture, and *objets d'art,* of which he never seemed to have enough.

The Marquis would have been inhuman if he had not been considerably flattered by this attention.

Besides, after the years of fighting, when he lost what amounted to his boyhood, there was the irresistible allure of the Beauties like Daisy, and a dozen others.

He had gone into the Army as soon as he left School.

It was therefore the first time he had come into contact with the "Cyprians," who were acknowledged to be the most attractive in Europe.

Even Paris could not compete with the loveliness of women like Letty Lesse.

Then there were "incomparables" who became the talk of the Clubs in St.

James's because they were new and unusual.

The Marquis had kept telling himself he should go to the country.

When he suggested it, his friends always had a good reason why he should stay for at least another week.

Now he felt guilty that he had neglected what was his most treasured possession.

He had been ruminating for more than half-an-hour, when Johnson opened the door and announced:

"Mr. Waters, M'Lord!"

Waters came into the room.

The Marquis, who had not seen him for years, was shocked by his appearance.

He had grown enormously fat, was red-faced and going bald.

When the Marquis had seen him last, he had been a fairly young man.

He had seemed, by the quickness with which he moved and his sharp brain, an ideal Estate Manager.

Now it was obvious that he drank too frequently and ate too well, on the proceeds, the Marquis thought, he had extorted out of the Estate.

The interview did not take long.

It was impossible for Waters to deny

that he had been helping himself for years by entering false information into the ledgers.

He was making money from men who were either dead or moving disconsolately about the village because they were unemployed.

The Marquis gave him exactly forty-eight hours in which to vacate his house and leave the County.

"I am not sending you to prison," he said in icy tones which seemed to cut like a whip, "but I want an account of what you have in your Bank and I will leave you just enough to prevent you from starving."

It was useless, Waters knew, to say anything.

His fat, florid face had gone very pale, and there was an expression of terror in his eyes.

When finally he left the room, he moved slowly, like an old man who could hardly control his feet.

The Marquis rose from his desk and walked to the window.

He looked out at the sun shining below on the lake.

He asked himself why, when everything in the world was so perfect, must people be so vile, greedy, and corrupt?

Then he remembered Christina saying there was a lot for him to do, and he knew it was true.

He sent for Johnson.

He ordered him to fetch the Head Gardener, the Head Groom, and the Head Game-Keeper to him immediately.

It took some time, but he saw them one by one.

He ordered them to employ every available man in the village, starting with those who had returned from the war.

He could see the excitement in their eyes as they responded to everything he suggested.

It was obvious this was something in which they had been hoping.

It was after four o'clock before he had finished.

Then he ordered a Phaeton.

As it came round to the front of the house, he told Johnson that he wanted six footmen in the hall.

He was to make sure that their livery fitted them properly.

He did not need to be told that Johnson had been kept short of foot-men in his absence.

Those who were there looked as if they

had quickly been taken on, once it was known he was on his way home.

The Marquis got into his Phaeton.

He drove down the drive and along the road to Four Gables.

He noticed as he had not done before that the garden was ablaze with flowers.

The shrubs were in bloom and several almond trees were in blossom.

When he reached the front-door he handed his reins to the groom who was beside him, and stepped down.

The front-door was open.

As he suspected, Christina did not have any servants, so he walked in.

He thought he would probably find her in the Sitting-Room and wondered which door that would be.

Even as he hesitated, he heard her scream.

For a second he thought he must have dreamt it.

Then he heard her say:

"No, no! Please . . . leave me . . . alone! Go . . . away!"

"That is something I have no intention of doing," a man's voice replied.

Just as the Marquis's hand went out towards the handle, Christina screamed again.

The Marquis walked into the room.

Christina was struggling against a man who was towering over her.

He had his back to the Marquis and he was pulling Christina close to him.

Although she was struggling desperately, she was far too small and fragile to be able to resist him.

"As the front-door was open," the Marquis said in a lofty tone, "I came in!"

The man who had his arms round Christina started and turned to face him.

It was then that Christina managed to struggle free.

Without thinking, but instinctively, she ran towards the Marquis and threw herself against him.

"S-Send him . . . away . . . please . . . send him . . . away," she begged.

The Marquis was staring at the man and recognised him.

He was a neighbour named Sir Mortimer Stinger.

He remembered how his Father had disliked him.

They had a long row for years over the ownership of some acres of land.

Sir Mortimer, who was a man of about forty and well known as a "womaniser," said, after a moment's silence:

"So you have decided to come home, have you, Melverley? Laden, no doubt, with the spoils of war."

"Yes, I have come home," the Marquis replied coldly. "I find there is a great deal for me to do to bring things back to the way they were when my Father was alive, and that, of course, includes you!"

The late Marquis had forbidden Sir Mortimer to set foot on his Estate, or have any further communication with him.

Sir Mortimer looked angry and retorted:

"You were always a very unpleasant small boy, in my opinion, Melverley, and I do not suppose you have changed with the years."

"Not where you are concerned," the Marquis said, "and as this house is on my Estate, I forbid you to come here again!"

"Do you really believe you can give me orders like that?" Sir Mortimer asked furiously. "This is a free country, and if I wish to visit Miss Churston, I shall certainly do so without your permission!"

He did not wait for the Marquis to reply, but walked past him to leave the room.

They heard his footsteps walking across the hall.

Christina, who had hidden her face in the Marquis's shoulder, moved, saying:

"Thank you . . . thank you! You came at just the . . . right moment . . . he was trying to . . . kiss me! I . . . I hate him . . . he is a . . . horrible man!"

"I agree with you," the Marquis said. "You must not see him again."

"I . . . I locked myself in the last few times he called," Christina said, "but Nanny has . . . gone to the village . . . and . . . and I thought it was . . . y-you."

"Have you no other servants here?" the Marquis enquired.

Christina moved away from him towards the fireplace.

She was blushing as she said:

"P-perhaps you do not . . . understand that things have been . . . very different since the war ended. Many of the county Banks . . . closed their doors . . . and that happened to the one in which . . . Papa kept his . . . money."

The Marquis moved across the room

to be nearer to her and sat down in a high-backed chair.

"I want you to tell me more about what has been happening," he said. "You were quite right about the Hall. I have discovered that Waters has been cheating the Estate, and I have given him forty-eight hours to leave the County."

Christina clasped her hands together.

"Have you really done that? Oh . . . thank you . . . thank you! He was a . . . horrible man and has . . . refused to employ any of the men who have come back from the war. He has not repaired the cottages . . . and has even reduced the pensions of the old people."

"I will see to it," the Marquis said, "but I think, Christina, you will have to help me. There must be many other things that have been going on. I cannot know about them unless you tell me what they are."

"I . . . will tell you . . . of course . . . I will tell you . . . now that you have got rid of Mr. Waters."

Christina sat down on the rug at his feet.

"Oh, I am so thankful that you are back!" she said. "I have prayed every night that you would not be away too long, as things got worse and worse . . . then I began to think that . . . perhaps you did not . . . care."

"How could you think that?" the Marquis asked.

At the same time, he had a little twinge of conscience as he thought of how much time he had wasted with Daisy and Letty.

"Now, suppose we start at the beginning," he said, "and you tell me how you have become involved with Stinger."

Christina looked shy.

"He . . . He . . . asked me to . . . marry him several months ago . . . and Papa told him he would . . . never sanction such a . . . union . . . and he was not to come here again. But after Papa . . . died . . . he started . . . coming back again."

She made a helpless little gesture with her hands.

The Marquis was aware of how much it had frightened her.

"What I want you to do," he said, "is to pack your things, and you and your Nurse must come and stay at the Hall."

Christina's eyes opened very wide.

"Come to the . . . Hall?" she queried.

"It is the only way I can be certain of

keeping Mortimer Stinger away," the Marquis explained. "He will not dare to come to the Hall, especially if I am there."

"That would be . . . wonderful!" Christina said. "But . . . I must not be a nuisance . . . or worse still . . . an encumbrance."

"You are going to help me, as you have promised to do," the Marquis said. "I want to put my Estate in order and, quite frankly, I have no wish to discuss it with the Vicar or anybody else except you. You put me on the right lines where Waters was concerned, and now you must help me cope with the other things."

He thought she looked a little indecisive, and added:

"If your Father were here, I know I could ask him. As it is, you have to take his place."

He saw by the expression on Christina's face that he had said exactly the right thing.

"Of course Papa would have . . . helped you," she said. "He took such an interest in the . . . Estate and often discussed it with . . . your Father."

"Then you have to discuss it with me,"

the Marquis said, "and as I have to move quickly so that there is no more suffering and no more unhappiness, you had better start packing."

Christina laughed.

"Can you really say it, just like that?"

"Of course," the Marquis said, "and what I am going to do is to take you back with me now in my Phaeton. Then we can settle down and work out exactly what is required in the village, on the Farms and on the Estate."

He paused before adding:

"I will send a carriage to collect your Nurse and your luggage and also someone to help her pack."

"You are so kind and thoughtful," Christina exclaimed. "I do not know of any other man who would think of that, and Nanny is growing old."

She gave a little sigh.

"That is why it worried me when we could not afford the women who worked in the house when Papa was alive. One does come in once a week, because I give her material she can make up for her children's clothes, but that was all."

"You told me your relations are in Northumberland," the Marquis said, "but is there no one else who could look after you?"

He was thinking as he spoke that it might be a mistake to have Christina at the Hall without a chaperon.

He had suffered so much from the gossips in London. If Christina was his guest, it would not escape the notice of those in the country.

As if she were following his thoughts, Christina said:

"Perhaps . . . as I have no chaperon . . . it would be a . . . mistake for me . . . to come. I will not . . . answer the door again . . . unless I am . . . certain it is . . . not Sir Mortimer."

"I want you at the Hall," the Marquis said firmly, "but I am, of course, thinking of your reputation."

Christina gave a little laugh.

"It is only people like Sir Mortimer who would say nasty things about me because I was not at home when he called."

The Marquis thought that was an understatement.

He was wondering if there was anybody in the neighbourhood who could chaperon her, when Christina said:

"If you are . . . really serious . . . about

my having a chaperon . . . Miss Dickson is still alive."

The Marquis stared at her.

"Miss Dickson?" he asked. "She must be a hundred!"

"She is not as old as that!" Christina laughed. "She is seventy."

Miss Dickson had been the Marquis's Governess when he was a little boy of seven.

Before that his Mother and his Nanny had taught him.

They then decided he should have lessons at regular hours every day.

Miss Dickson, who was the daughter of a Bishop, had been their choice.

The Marquis remembered he had been very fond of her.

She was a plain woman, but she had a great sense of humour.

She had taught him his first lessons extremely well.

She had also given him, he knew later, a desire to teach himself by studying the right books.

Looking back, he could remember how she had made history come alive for him.

During the war, other Nations joined Wellington in the effort to defeat Napoleon.

It was then he remembered the things Miss Dickson had told him about the Germans, the Austrians, and the Russians.

Whether he was fighting beside them or, after Napoleon's defeat, meeting them in Paris, it was due to Miss Dickson that he understood them.

Eagerly he asked now:

"Where is Miss Dickson?"

"She lives in the cottage your Father gave her," Christina replied, "but it is in very bad repair. The roof leaks and although I pleaded with Mr. Waters, he would do nothing about it."

The Marquis frowned.

"That man ought to be shot!" he said. "How dare he refuse to do anything for Miss Dickson!"

"He refused to do anything for anybody," Christina said, "but I know she will be thrilled to come to the Hall and perhaps . . ."

Christina looked at the Marquis anxiously:

". . . perhaps you could have . . . her cottage repaired . . . while she is not in it."

"It will be the first one to be done!" the Marquis said firmly.

Christina gave a little cry of joy and he added:

"Surely you realise that you and I are going to tidy up the whole place, and make certain that everyone is happy? There will not be a person in the whole of the village who is unemployed, unless he wants to be!"

Christina clapped her hands together.

"That is exactly what we want. Oh, thank you, thank you! How can you be so . . . wonderful! You have come just . . . when we were beginning to . . . despair."

"I should have come before," the Marquis said.

Christina was not listening.

She had jumped up and was running to the door.

The Marquis was aware that while they had been talking there had been a sound outside in the hall.

Then he heard Christina cry:

"Nanny, what do you think? His Lordship is here, and we are going . . . to stay at the Hall . . . and everything is going to be . . . perfect again, just like it was in the . . . old days when Papa and Mama . . . were alive, and everybody was . . . happy!"

The excitement in Christina's voice was very moving.

As the Marquis joined her, he saw that she was talking to an elderly woman with grey hair.

She looked, he thought, exactly as a Nanny should look.

He held out his hand and Nanny curtsied.

"I'm that glad . . . Your Lordship's . . . back!" she said.

There was just a note in her voice as if she would like to have added:

"And about time too!"

The Marquis was reminded of his own Nanny. It was what she would have said.

"As Miss Christina has told you," he said, "I have invited you both to the Hall to help me get things straight. Christina and I are going to call on Miss Dickson to see if she will leave her leaking cottage and come with us too."

Nanny stared at the Marquis as if she could not believe her ears.

Then she said:

"You're a real Gentleman, M'Lord, just like your Father, and now that 'orrible war's over, we needs you here."

"Go and pack your clothes, Nanny,"

61

the Marquis said as he smiled. "I am sending a carriage and someone to help you."

There was a sudden glitter of tears in Nanny's eyes.

The Marquis knew how desperately worried she must have been about the lack of money, and also Christina's involvement with Sir Mortimer Stinger.

Nanny's next words confirmed that this was the truth.

"I saw that unpleasant Gentleman's carriage going through the village as I was coming back," she said to Christina. "Has he been here again?"

"His Lordship saved me, Nanny," Christina answered.

"I told you not to open the door!" Nanny said sharply.

"I did not know it was him," Christina said. "In fact, I thought it was His Lordship."

"He will not trouble her again," the Marquis interposed firmly. "Just as my Father would not allow him on the Estate, I will do the same!"

He saw the relief in Nanny's eyes, and added:

"Do not worry. She will be safe enough

at the Hall. There will be plenty of people there to look after her."

"I'm thanking God, M'Lord," Nanny said fervently, "that you've come just in the nick of time!"

chapter three

The Marquis helped Christina into his Phaeton.

Then, as he drove off, he said:

"I think we will call on Miss Dickson on the way. You must tell me which cottage she is in."

"It is right at the very end of the village," Christina answered. "It was very pretty when she first went into it, but nothing has been done to it for a long time. The thatched roof needs repairing and the windows painting, but Mr. Waters would not listen, even when Papa spoke to him."

The Marquis did not say anything.

But Christina was aware that his lips tightened, and she knew how angry it made him.

"Now that you are . . . back," she said in a soft voice, "I know that . . . everything will be . . . different."

"It will take time," the Marquis said, "but the most important thing is to employ the men who fought so bravely in the war."

"That is what Papa thought about those who grew up during it," Christina said, "but when the Farmers on the Estate asked for them, Mr. Waters would not allow them to employ any more men than they had already."

The Marquis could explain the reason why, but he thought it was a mistake.

He wanted to forget what had happened and concentrate on what should be done immediately.

Christina pointed out to him the cottage in which Miss Dickson was living.

He could see that it had once been very attractive.

Now the gate was off its hinges, the door and the windows had not been painted, and the whole cottage looked dilapidated.

The groom went to the horses' heads and the Marquis helped Christina out of the Phaeton.

As they walked up the path to the front-door, she said in a whisper:

"This is going to be very exciting for Miss Dickson! She has been . . . longing for . . . you to come . . . home."

The Marquis knocked on the door, and a voice he knew said:

"Come in!"

He opened it.

Miss Dickson, looking very much

65

older and somehow smaller, was sitting by the fire.

Her hair was white and there were lines on her face he did not remember.

At the same time, her smile when she saw him was just as it had always been.

"It is you, Master Mervy!" she exclaimed. "You are back!"

"Yes, I am back, Dickie," the Marquis said, "and I know you are going to say — 'better late than never!' "

Miss Dickson laughed.

"It seems a very long time since you went away, but God has heard my prayers, and you have come back safe and sound!"

"That is true," the Marquis said, "and now I want your help."

Miss Dickson looked surprised.

"I have just rescued Christina," the Marquis said, "from that abominable man, Sir Mortimer Stinger. I am taking her and her Nurse to the Hall, but as you will understand, she must be chaperoned."

The twinkle in the Marquis's eyes was echoed by that in Miss Dickson's.

"Of course!" she said demurely. "And if those are your orders, My Lord, I am only too willing to oblige."

The Marquis laughed outright.

"They are not my orders, Dickie. You were the one who gave those, but we need you to help me put right things that have gone badly wrong since my Father died."

"They have indeed," Miss Dickson agreed in a serious voice, "but if you dealt with Napoleon, you can certainly deal with what has happened on the Melverley Estate."

"I will do my best," the Marquis said, "but I need both you and Christina to assist me."

Miss Dickson smiled at him, and he said:

"I will send a carriage to collect you in an hour's time. I expect you can be ready by then?"

"I shall not only be ready, but waiting impatiently," Miss Dickson replied. "It is the most exciting thing that has happened to me since I was first made your Governess when you were seven years old!"

There was a moving note of sincerity in her voice.

The Marquis thought how much she must have disliked being pensioned off in a cottage.

She had ruled the Schoolroom with "a rod of iron" for so many years.

A quick glance round the room showed him that the paper was peeling off the walls and damp was percolating through the ceiling.

The floor-boards creaked ominously when he walked across them.

"Well, hurry, Dickie," he said, "and get packed. Christina and I need you, and we cannot afford to waste any time."

"It is just like old times to hear you talking like that," Miss Dickson said. "You always were in a hurry and would never listen when I told you 'More haste, less speed.'"

The Marquis laughed.

Christina bent and kissed Miss Dickson.

"Everything is going to be . . . wonderful now that His Lordship is . . . back," she said, "and he is taking Nanny and me to the Hall to . . . escape from that . . . horrible Sir Mortimer."

"That man is a menace!" Miss Dickson said angrily.

"He will not come again now that I am home," the Marquis said reassuringly, "but I think Christina will be safer at the Hall with you and Nurse to look after her."

"Of course she will," Miss Dickson agreed, "but, all the same, Sir Mortimer is a nasty man, and there are many unpleasant tales told about his behaviour in the County."

"I wish we could be rid of him," the Marquis said, "but there are more important things to be done first."

He took Christina back to the Phaeton.

Miss Dickson managed to get to her feet to wave good-bye to them as they left.

"Is she really ill?" the Marquis asked.

"I think if she had good food and a house that is not damp so that it affected her rheumatism, she would be just like her old self," Christina answered.

The Marquis wanted to say how angry it made him to think that anyone who had meant so much in his life should be left in such appalling conditions.

He was wise enough, however, to know it was no use going on thinking about Waters's wickedness.

What he had to do was to get the wheels turning in the other direction.

He had already made a note of the cottages in the village that were to be seen to immediately.

They reached the Hall.

The Marquis gave Johnson orders that a carriage was to be sent to Four Gables for Nanny and the luggage, and also to pick up Miss Dickson.

"I do not expect they will be here for at least another hour," he added, "so tell the Chef that dinner is to be later than usual."

He remembered that his Father had dined at seven o'clock.

In London the Prince Regent had made it fashionable to dine later.

It was sometimes nine o'clock before His Royal Highness sat down at the table.

While the Marquis was giving his orders, Christina had gone ahead into the room at the end of the hall.

She had always thought it was the prettiest room she had ever seen.

It had a big bow window looking out over the garden at the back.

She also loved the exquisitely carved fireplace which had been put in when the house was renovated during the last century.

It was Robert Adam who had done the restoration.

He had managed to keep some of the older rooms the same as they were in Tudor times.

At the same time, he had made the house extremely impressive with a new facade.

He added East and West wings to the main building.

It had increased its size and importance, and, in Christina's eyes, its beauty.

But she still liked some of the older rooms with their low ceilings.

She enjoyed, too, the twisting staircases and the secret passages in which she had played ever since she was a small child.

As she looked round the room, she thought Melverley Hall was a Fairy Palace with a magic all its own.

When the Marquis had given his orders, he joined her.

"Now, where shall we start?" he asked. "You have already told me two things of importance — that Waters was crooked and that almost every cottage in the village is in need of repair."

"Perhaps you feel you have done

enough for one day," Christina said as she smiled.

"Now you are underestimating my powers of endurance," the Marquis replied.

He went to an exquisite *Secrétaire* in the corner of the room and brought back some crested writing-paper and a pen.

"Now, tell me what else needs doing," he said.

Christina immediately began a list of Farms which should have made a reasonable profit like most other Farms during the war.

But they had been deprived of workmen, of implements, and livestock.

"The Farmers begged Mr. Waters almost on their knees to be allowed to cultivate more land," Christina said, "but he always refused."

Christina paused for a moment before continuing:

"Now, as I expect you know, the bottom has fallen out of the market and the Farmers are having a very hard time."

The Marquis had in fact heard this in London.

He had, however, imagined that

everything was well at Melverley.

Now he knew he had to learn a great deal about what was saleable and what was not.

And he must certainly restock the Farms with chickens, cows, and sheep.

He had also to decide what crops would be most in demand in the market.

"Things have been very, very bad," Christina said in her soft voice, "because, on top of everything else, there was a disastrous harvest last year."

The Marquis then learnt that the large kitchen gardens had been neglected.

This meant that most of the village was without vegetables.

Even potatoes, which in many large families were the staple diet, were unobtainable.

It had always been understood that the Big House provided vegetables for the whole village at a reduced cost.

The Marquis did not need to be told that a large number of the villagers had gone hungry.

They had been unable to afford meat or chickens, and there were no longer the vegetables on which they had always relied.

He had already given his Head Gardener permission to employ as many men as were necessary.

The situation, therefore, would soon re-adjust itself.

At the same time, he made a note to send to the nearest market for vegetables and see that they were available in the village shop.

There were so many things to talk about.

It was with a start that Christina realised that it was nearly time to dress for dinner.

"I must go upstairs and find out which room Mrs. Dartford has prepared for me."

The Marquis remembered that this was the name of his Housekeeper, and he said quickly:

"I, too, must come and see her. I know now I should have gone to see the Kitchen staff before I returned to your house. But I brought my Chef in London with me, and did not think of it."

"I am sure they will forgive you if you go and see them now," Christina said, "and I know they will all want to say how glad they are to have you back."

Mrs. Dartford curtsied to the Marquis,

at the same time leaving him in no doubt as to what her feelings were when he went down to the Kitchen.

Mrs. Boswin, the Cook, had been there since before he was born.

She was getting old, but she had managed, she told him, to keep going, although she was having trouble with her legs.

"I am looking forward to your gingerbread biscuits, Mrs. Boswin," the Marquis said.

Mrs. Boswin laughed.

"You was always a greedy little boy when it come to me cooking," she answered, "but I hears now you 'ardly eats enough to keep a mouse alive!"

"That is not quite true," the Marquis said, laughing. "But I like to ride light, and you know as well as I do that too many gingerbread biscuits can put on pounds."

"Nevertheless, Oi'll make them for you, M'Lord, an' it'll be me heart that's singin', even if me legs won't carry me!"

The Marquis looked round the huge Kitchen with its large stoves.

He could remember seeing hanging from the beams every sort of game fowl besides haunches of ham and long strings of onions.

He told himself he must soon make it look as it used to do.

As if Mrs. Boswin were following his thoughts, she said:

"It makes me blood boil, M'Lord, when I thinks o' the days when there was so much food, we could 'ardly eat it all. But these past years there was a 'ole in all our tummies, as you used to say when you were a little lad."

"I am sure, Mrs. Boswin, I shall not say that again," the Marquis replied. "I am looking forward to dinner."

"O'll do somethin' special for you this evening," Mrs. Boswin replied, " 'though o' course Your Lordship's brought down a fancy Chef with you from London."

The Marquis realised this was a sore point and something he should not have done.

He therefore said quickly:

"It was only a precaution, Mrs. Boswin. I was not sure if there would be anybody here to cook for me. I will send the Chef back to London as soon as you have no further need of him."

He saw the light come into Mrs. Boswin's eyes.

She had not, as she thought, been usurped by a "foreigner" from London.

As the Marquis left the Kitchen, he saw his London Chef and another man whom he knew was his assistant going towards the Kitchen.

He stopped them and said to the Chef:

"Mrs. Boswin has been here ever since I was born, and I thought perhaps she had retired, otherwise I would not have brought you here with me. Be as tactful as you can and let her cook any dish she pleases."

The Chef, who was a sensible man, nodded.

"I understands, M'Lord."

"I was sure you would," the Marquis replied, "and as you know, the people who have lived here for so many years think of this as their home."

The Chef nodded in agreement.

The Marquis hurried back to the front of the house and up to his bedroom.

Yates was waiting for him, and he said as the Marquis entered:

"You've caused a flutter, and no mistake, M'Lord, they're talkin' 'bout you as if you were an Archangel from Heaven wot's dropped down amongst 'em!"

The Marquis smiled.

He was used to Yates commenting on everything that happened in his life.

It had often cheered him up during the war when they had been in a particularly tricky situation.

Even when they had to camp out without shelter on a windy Portuguese mountain, Yates's good humour had never failed him.

The Marquis allowed him liberties he would not have tolerated with any other servant.

He had the Marquis's bath ready.

In her bedroom further down the corridor, Christina was enjoying hers.

It had been put in front of the fire and the warm water was scented by something Mrs. Dartford had put in it.

"I remember that scent!" Christina exclaimed when her bath was ready.

"I've got two bottles of it stored away," Mrs. Dartford answered, "which I was keepin' for a special occasion. An' what could be more special than th' day His Lordship comes home to us?"

"What indeed!" Christina agreed. "I know everything is going to be exactly as it was when I first came here as a little girl."

"And a very pretty one you was too!"

Mrs. Dartford said. "I can remember your Mother, God rest her, bringing you wi' her when you could only just walk. An' when you got older you used t'play *'Hide and Seek'* with th' young house-maids."

"I can remember doing that," Christina said, and laughed.

"It's somethin' perhaps your chil-dren'll do when you've got them," Mrs. Dartford said.

Christina looked at her and she added:

"His Lordship's given orders that I'm to have as many housemaids as I needs to help me in the house. That's a real relief, as it had got down to just me an' Emily."

"I am sure every young girl in the village will want to come here," Christina said.

Mrs. Dartford laughed.

"News of what's bin 'appening 'as gone through the village like wildfire!" she said. "Already we've had four girls knocking on the back door, beggin' me to employ them."

"You must employ them all!" Christina said. "The house is so big and His Lordship wants it to look exactly as

79

it did when his Mother was alive."

"I knows that," Mrs. Dartford said. "I only hopes I can put them to work before His Lordship sees the mess the Picture Gallery's in, an' the rooms on the Second Floor haven't seen a duster for years!"

There was a note of elation in her voice which told Christina how exciting it was for her to have new house-maids.

She would get them to make the house shine as it had in the old days, as if it were a precious jewel.

Nanny and Mrs. Dartford helped Christina into a pretty but simple evening gown.

The mere simplicity of it was a perfect frame for her curly golden hair and the clearness of her eyes.

Christina, however, felt like the Beggar-maid at the Court of King Cophetua.

Then she told herself sensibly:

"His Lordship will not be looking at what I am wearing, but listening to what I have to tell him."

Mrs. Dartford was looking at her critically.

"What you wants to freshen up that

gown," she said slowly, "be a few flowers — some at th' waist, an' one or two at the back of your head."

She went from the bedroom.

A vase of flowers had been hastily arranged outside in the corridor.

Mrs. Dartford pinned a white rose and some lilies of the valley at Christina's waist, and attached two roses to the back of her head.

Looking at herself in the mirror, Christina had to admit that it made a difference.

"Thank you, thank you!" she exclaimed. "You have been very kind."

Because she was eager to be with the Marquis again, she ran from the room.

He was waiting for her at the bottom of the staircase.

In his evening-clothes, she thought that no man could look smarter, or more impressive.

His cravat was tied in an intricate fashion, and the points of his collar were high.

As she walked towards him, he thought how graceful she was.

He was wondering how she would look if he could dress her as he had dressed Letty, choosing for her the best gowns from the most expensive shops in Bond Street.

Then he told himself that Christina was only a child.

It would be a great mistake for her to become self-conscious about her appearance.

When she reached him and they walked into the Drawing-Room together, he said:

"Miss Dickson has arrived, but as the excitement of it all has been too much for her, I suggested she go to bed. So you must, in consequence, dine alone with me."

Christina could not help thinking with a leap of her heart that she would much rather be alone with him, fond though she was of Miss Dickson.

Aloud she said:

"Should I run up and see if there is anything I can do for her?"

"I am sure my staff will look after her very well," the Marquis replied, "and the same dinner that will be served to us will be taken upstairs to her."

"I hope she is not ill!" Christina said. "She was not at all well last winter, but that was because her cottage is damp."

The Marquis did not say anything, and she went on:

"But I am sure now that she is here, she will be well taken care of and will soon be as active as she used to be."

"She was always very active," the Marquis replied. "I can remember her taking me on long walks when I would much rather have ridden."

"I expect you did that too," Christina said.

She gave a little sigh.

"When your Father, the late Marquis, was alive, he used to allow me to ride the horses in his stables, but after he died, Mr. Waters sold most of them."

"Horses must certainly go on the list of things to be replaced," the Marquis said. "I shall visit the sale room at the first opportunity."

He saw the question in Christina's eyes and added:

"You can ride them whenever you like."

"Oh, thank you . . . thank you," Christina cried. "I was hoping you would say that. I love riding! And with Ben dead and empty stables, I have no-one to pull the pony-cart."

"As you are here, you will not need that for the moment," the Marquis remarked. "You will have to help me get some carriage horses as well as those we are to ride."

"I believe there is a Horse Fair taking place at the beginning of next week," Christina said.

The Marquis was interested.

They found themselves talking about horses all during the first part of the meal.

When dinner was over, they went into the Drawing-Room.

The servants were no longer there, and once again the Marquis was asking what needed doing.

They had made a long list, when the door opened and Johnson came in.

He came over to the Marquis's side and said:

"There's a Gentleman here, M'Lord, asking to see you."

"At this time of night?" the Marquis exclaimed.

"I understands, M'Lord, he's bin involved in an accident, otherwise he'd have got here earlier. But he and his Valet are now waiting your instructions in the Morning-Room."

"Who is it, Johnson?" the Marquis enquired.

"The Gentleman says he's a member of your family an' his name be Mr. Terence Verley."

The Marquis considered this for a moment, then said:

"If his name is Verley, he must be one of the family, but I do not remember him. Well, I suppose you had better bring him in."

"Very good, M'Lord."

Johnson left the room and the Marquis turned to Christina:

"Have you ever heard of Terence Verley?"

"If I am not mistaken," she replied, "he is the son of your Father's younger brother, but for some reason he was not welcome at the family parties."

The Marquis raised his eye-brows, but before he could make any comment, Johnson announced:

"Mr. Terence Verley, M'Lord."

A man came into the Drawing-Room. Christina saw at once that he was dressed in the height of fashion.

In fact, his cravat was almost too high and too elaborate.

His coat looked too square on his shoulders, and his Hessians were over-polished.

He walked up to the Marquis with outstretched hands.

"My dear Cousin," he exclaimed, "let me welcome you back from the wars! It has been a long time since we met, but I am only hoping you have not forgotten me."

"As you say," the Marquis remarked, "it has been a long time."

"I have thought about you so often," Terence Verley went on, "but I was sure that, somehow, with your usual good luck you would survive Napoleon's cannon balls."

"I did my best," the Marquis said, "and, as you see, have managed to survive unscathed."

"It must have been terrible — terrible!" Terence Verley exclaimed. "But now you are back — and master of all you survey!"

He glanced around the room as he spoke.

"It may sound rude," the Marquis remarked, "but I cannot remember you. Did you stay here as a boy?"

"I am afraid not," Terence Verley admitted. "Our fathers — stupid old men — quarrelled, and I was barred from the house. Anyway, why should we worry about ancient feuds?"

"Why indeed," the Marquis answered. "May I offer you some refreshment?"

As if he had anticipated this was what Terence Verley would want, Johnson came in with a bottle of champagne.

He was followed by a footman carrying a tray on which there were three glasses.

"You must allow me to drink to your health and to your most successful homecoming!" Terence Verley said.

He raised his glass of champagne which had just been poured out and said:

"To a great warrior and — far more important — the Head of the Melverley family!"

"Thank you," the Marquis said.

He took a sip of the champagne while Terence Verley emptied his glass in a theatrical fashion and held it out to be refilled.

Then, as he would have sat down, the Marquis said:

"Do I understand that you have travelled here specially to see me, or are you staying in the neighbourhood?"

"I am hoping you will be generous enough to accommodate me for the night," Terence Verley replied. "I have in fact made the journey to see you — on business."

"On business?" the Marquis queried.

Because of the way he accentuated the words, Christina rose to her feet.

"I think," she said, "as it is growing late, I should go and see how Miss Dickson is, then go to bed."

"That is sensible of you," the Marquis agreed, "because we have a lot to do to-morrow."

"You have done a great deal already," Christina said softly, "and a great many people are going to bed to-night very happy."

"I hope that is true. Good-night, Christina," the Marquis replied.

She dropped him a graceful curtsy.

"Good-night, My Lord, and thank you for all your kindness."

She went toward Terence Verley, who was staring at her.

"We have not been introduced," he said, "but may I tell you that you are very beautiful! You shine in this room like a star in the sable of the night sky!"

It sounded poetical, but at the same time, Christina felt a little embarrassed.

There was something in his expression she did not like.

She had the feeling that whatever business he might wish to do with the Marquis, it would be only to his personal advantage.

Terence Verley held out his hand, but she pretended not to have seen it.

"Good-night, Sir," she said, and hurried to the door.

The Marquis opened it for her.

"Thank you . . . again," she said softly so that only he could hear.

Then she was hurrying across the hall and up the staircase.

The Marquis shut the door.

As he walked back he noticed that Terence Verley was helping himself to a third glass of champagne.

"Now we are alone," the Marquis said, "I think you had better tell me exactly why you are here and what your business is."

"That is quite easy," Terence Verley replied. "I am, now that my Father is dead, your Heir Presumptive, and what I want, my dear Cousin, is money! In fact, to put it bluntly, I need ten thousand pounds!"

chapter four

There was a pregnant silence.

Then the Marquis asked:

"Is this a joke?"

"On the contrary," Terence Verley replied, "I am very serious. It is a case of either going to a Debtors' Prison, which would create a family scandal, or you help me."

Very quietly the Marquis said:

"I think you had better explain first how you can be my Heir Presumptive."

"It is not difficult," Terence Verley answered, "but you might not like what you hear."

He helped himself to another glass of champagne.

Then he sat down in a comfortable armchair, apparently at his ease.

The Marquis stood in front of the fireplace, waiting.

"My Father," Terence Verley said finally, "was the third son of the second Marquis. He was apparently a dashing young man, which does not surprise me, but there was practically no money and he had to make his own way in the world."

"What did he do?" the Marquis enquired.

"He enjoyed himself in London until his debts became so large that no-one would give him credit. He then married a rich heiress."

"That sounds a sensible thing to have done," the Marquis said. "I suppose she paid his debts."

"She paid them willingly because he was a Verley, or, rather, her Father did!"

The Marquis asked the question without putting it into words.

There was a mocking twist to Terence Verley's lips as he said:

"One could hardly expect the family to approve, but her Father was an extremely skilful Ship Owner who made a fortune out of carrying slaves from Africa to America to work in the cotton fields."

The Marquis stiffened.

He could think of nothing more revolting than the trafficking of slaves.

He could understand all too well that the family would be horrified at such a trade.

"As you can imagine," Terence Verley went on, "my Father was kicked out of the family, and I understand my Grand-father's name was never mentioned."

"I can understand that they would be upset by your Father's marriage," the Marquis said.

"I was brought up in luxury, but of course without the approval or support of the blue-blooded Verleys," Terence said. "My Father lived to a great age. In fact, he died only two months ago at the age of ninety-five."

"Certainly an unusually long life," the Marquis remarked.

"Unfortunately, having survived his father-in-law by twenty-five years, the money he enjoyed through his marriage had come to an end. That is why I am now in debt, just as he was."

Terence Verley spread out his hands dramatically as he said:

"I am therefore turning to the only person who can help me, and that, of course, is you."

"And you really think that I should support you?" the Marquis asked.

"Why not?" Terence enquired. "Now that my Father is dead, I am your Heir Presumptive, and I cannot imagine you would want to see the future Marquis of Melverley behind bars."

"How old are you?" the Marquis asked unexpectedly.

"I am thirty-two," Terence replied.

"You realise, of course, that there is every chance of my having a son, maybe even two or three, before I die?"

"I have taken that into account," Terence said. "At the same time, I consider it your duty to prevent me from going to prison, and to make sure, as a member of the family, that I do not starve to death in the future."

The Marquis, who was a very good judge of men, realised Terence Verley was putting on an extremely good act.

But he was aware that the man who was making this extraordinary proposition to him was nervous.

The Marquis was thinking quickly.

At the same time, he himself appeared to be completely unmoved by his Cousin's dramatics.

He merely appeared to be considering what he had said, carefully and conscientiously.

"How did you get here?" he asked.

"I came in a Post Chaise from London which, incidentally, I cannot pay," Terence answered.

"I will see to that," the Marquis said,

"and I think, as you have had a long journey and I have had a very busy day, we should go to bed and continue this conversation to-morrow morning."

"I would prefer to have your answer at once," Terence replied.

"Even if I wished to do so," the Marquis answered, "it would be difficult without consulting the family solicitors and of course examining the debts in detail so that they can be paid not by you, but by those who administer the family fortune on my behalf."

Terence laughed.

"You are afraid I might abscond with the money and leave you with the debts. All right, Cousin Mervyn, I concede a point there. But you must be aware of the consequences if you throw me to the wolves."

He drank down his champagne and rose to his feet.

"I beg you to think of the family," he said, "and how the name of Verley has been respected and admired all down the centuries."

The Marquis made no reply, and Terence laughed, but the sound had no humour in it.

"All right," he said, "so I am the 'Black

Sheep' of the family, and every family has one! But I cannot believe that ten thousand pounds is too large an amount for one of the heroes of Waterloo to find."

There was no denying the sneer in his voice as he spoke.

"You did not join the Army during the war?" the Marquis enquired.

"Good Heavens, no!" Terence replied. "I have no wish to go around shooting 'Frenchies.' They have never done me any harm. In fact, I find their food and their women extremely attractive!"

The Marquis realised that he was being provocative.

Walking towards the door, he said:

"I think we should both sleep on this problem."

"Unless you murder me during the night, it will be there to-morrow morning," Terence answered.

Pausing for a moment, he added:

"Quite frankly, I am delighted to have a bed that I do not have to pay for. The same applies to the champagne."

He filled his glass again and, carrying it in his hand, followed the Marquis, who had already left the room.

In the hall Johnson was waiting, and the Marquis said:

"Pay the driver of the Post Chaise in which Mr. Verley arrived and tell his Valet he will be staying the night."

"I've already done that, M'Lord," Johnson said. "Th' driver had to get back to London an' didn't want to wait."

"Then you realised that Mr. Verley will be staying the night," the Marquis said.

"Rooms have been arranged for him and his Valet, M'Lord," Johnson said, "and the luggage has already gone upstairs."

Terence Verley heard the end of this conversation.

He drank the champagne he carried and handed his glass to Johnson.

The Marquis, without saying any more, walked up the stairs.

When they reached the landing, he saw a man whom he guessed to be Terence Verley's Valet standing at an open door.

He turned to his Cousin.

"Good-night, Terence," he said, "I trust you sleep well. I shall endeavour to do the same."

"I am sure you will succeed," Terence answered.

There was an unpleasant sneer in his voice, but the Marquis walked on to the Master Suite.

It was at the end of the corridor.

It was where the Master of Melverley had slept since the house had been built in Tudor times by the first Earl of Verley.

When the Marquis reached it, he found, as he expected, that Yates was waiting for him.

The Valet shut the door and said, before the Marquis could speak:

"Well, this be a 'nice kettle of fish,' M'Lord, an' one we didn't expect."

"Are you referring to Mr. Terence Verley?" the Marquis enquired.

"Yes and 'is Valet, if you can call some Cockney straight aht th' gutter by that name!" Yates replied.

The Marquis knew that Yates should not speak in such a way of a member of his family.

But Yates had spoken his mind ever since they fought, particularly in Portugal, and made a perilous advance into France.

He invariably had something new and original to say about everything that happened.

He made the Marquis laugh in circumstances in which any other man would have felt like crying.

Now, as the Marquis undressed, he knew that Yates was as good a judge of people as he was himself.

He had never known him to make a mistake.

"Oi've 'eard abaht Mr. Terence," Yates went on, "from th' servants 'ere, an' they've not got a good word t' say abaht 'im."

"You have heard about him?" the Marquis exclaimed in surprise.

"Not only does 'e turn up 'ere unasked, M'Lord," Yates went on, "but Mr. Johnson told me abaht 'im an' 'is Father. 'E remembers 'ow the old Marquis 'ad 'im painted aht o' the Family Tree."

The Marquis realised that this was another reason why he had never heard of his Cousin Terence.

At the same time, he was asking himself what he could do about him.

He knew as clearly as if it had been said aloud that ten thousand pounds would be a mere "drop in the ocean."

If he paid up now, in less than a year Terence would be back for more.

It would mean a tremendous drain on his finances with all the expense of restoring the Estate.

The Marquis had been well aware

before he inherited that he would be responsible for a large number of the Verley relatives.

There were Aunts, Uncles, Cousins, and a maternal Grandmother.

All of them received a sum of money every year to enable them to live in comfort.

Besides this, there were innumerable pensioners, both at Melverley and in London, where there was some property he now owned.

This applied also to Leicestershire and to Newmarket.

Having inherited while he had been abroad, he had instructed the Solicitors, with regard to all these people, to carry on exactly as his Father had done.

He included the financing of the Alms Houses and Schools.

It all came, he was well aware, to an enormous sum of money.

But he had not yet since his arrival home had time to go into the whole business in detail.

He was confident that the Firm had carried out his instructions.

He knew now that he must find out exactly what was available.

He knew where he himself was concerned, he must not overspend so that any of the recipients suffered.

When he got into bed he found it difficult to sleep.

After coping with the mess Mr. Waters had made of everything, the last thing he needed was a disreputable, demanding Cousin.

He resented having to part with huge sums of money.

He was quite sure they would go the way the rest of Terence's money had gone.

It was only by using his will-power that he finally fell asleep.

As usual, the Marquis was called early.

When he went down to breakfast, it was to find Christina already there.

It was a sunlit room which faced south.

The sideboard was laden with silver *entrée* dishes containing the excellent food that the Marquis remembered from his childhood.

Christina smiled at him as he entered the room, and he said:

"Good-morning, Christina. I hope you slept well."

"I am so happy to be here," she said, "that for some time I could only sit thinking how beautiful my room was and how lucky you are to be looked after and protected by the ghosts of your family."

The Marquis laughed.

"Do you really believe in ghosts?"

"Of course I do," Christina answered, "and you must remember the 'White Lady,' who is the ghost of the Countess Sylvia. She is seen only if there is danger. Then the 'Black Knight' appears to drive it away."

"Now I am remembering," the Marquis exclaimed. "Dickie told me that story when I was a little boy and I used to peep over the bannisters hoping to see the 'Black Knight.' "

He helped himself from the dishes on the sideboard before he added:

"I was not so interested in those days in the 'White Lady,' but now, if she is very lovely, I shall be looking for her."

"To tell you there is danger?" Christina asked.

"Not exactly danger," the Marquis replied, "but a difficult problem."

He wondered if he should tell Christina about Terence, then decided it would be a mistake.

He therefore said, to change the subject:

"Where do you suggest we should go this morning, on our errand of mercy?"

"To the Farms!" Christina said at once. "I was so afraid you would want to put it off, with your Cousin here."

"I have no intention of doing that," the Marquis said, "and as he has not appeared for breakfast, I suspect he will emulate the Bucks in London, who, because they drink so deeply the previous night, seldom appear until it is time for luncheon."

"Then we can go to the Farms alone!" Christina said eagerly.

"I have absolutely no intention of taking my Cousin with us," the Marquis said sharply.

She knew from the way he spoke that Terence Verley had upset him.

She was too tactful, however, to ask questions.

She talked only about the Farmers, telling the Marquis who they were and how the only help they got came from their own families.

"Even the small children had to help bring in the harvest," she said, "because

Mr. Waters refused to allow them to employ any more people. Their wives were wonderful! I think they would be very thrilled if you told them so."

"Of course I will," the Marquis said, and smiled.

Finishing his breakfast, he rose from the table.

"I have ordered two horses," he said.

"I see you were sensible enough to put on a riding-habit."

"I knew it would be quicker to ride across country than to drive," Christina said, "but I would, of course, have changed if you had insisted on going in style."

The Marquis smiled at her.

"I have every intention of riding," he said, "and I hope the horse that is ready for you will come up to your expectations."

Christina laughed.

"I am overjoyed to have anything on four legs!" she answered.

She put on the jacket of her habit which she had left on a chair in the hall.

Her hat was there, too, which, despite being old, the Marquis thought very becoming.

He lifted Christina onto the saddle of a spirited bay while he himself mounted a black stallion.

He had ordered both horses to be brought down from London several weeks ago.

They rode off.

Because Christina knew the way better than he did, she led him through the paddock and on to some flat rough land.

The Marquis thought angrily it should have been cultivated during the war.

But it was a lovely day. The sun was shining which meant it would be hot later on.

Now there was a cool wind and, without speaking, they galloped their horses in order to take the friskiness out of them.

The Marquis noted, as he had expected, that Christina rode extremely well.

When she looked at him she could see that he seemed part of his horse and was an equestrian of whom her Father would have approved.

They spent a long time at the first Farm while the Farmer aired his grievances.

Christina was aware that the Marquis was a sympathetic listener.

She knew that was exactly what the Farmer required after having his troubles and difficulties brushed aside by Mr. Waters.

They sat in the farmhouse with its beamed ceiling.

The Farmer's wife brought them glasses of homemade cider.

Only when the Farmer had finished relating the story of his problems did the Marquis tell him what he could do about them.

The happiness on the faces of both the Farmer and his wife seemed to light up the whole room.

"D'ye mean that, M'Lord? D'ye really mean it?"

"I mean it," the Marquis said. "You can buy new stock, repair the buildings, and replace your worn-out implements. The sooner the better, if we are to get things done before the Winter."

"Ah can do it, M'Lord, now Ah've yer permission," the Farmer said.

It was then that Christina was aware there were tears running down his wife's cheeks.

"Ah' don' believe it!" she kept saying.

"Ah' don' believe it, after all we've bin through these long years, seein' our stock die an' unable to replace 'em. This can't be true!"

"It is true," Christina said comfortingly, "and I promise you everything will be different now that His Lordship has come home."

They left the farmhouse aware that the two people in it were looking years younger and so happy that their faces were transformed.

The same thing happened at the next Farm, and the next.

When finally they turned for home, Christina knew they were very late for luncheon.

"I tell you what we will do," the Marquis said. "As I do not feel like facing my Cousin Terence at the moment, and there is still more of the Estate to see, we will go to the *Fox and Duck*, and eat whatever they have to offer."

Christina laughed.

"You still remember that old Inn?"

"I remember them having a Meet there the first time I was allowed to go out hunting," the Marquis said. "I had a long ride, was in at the kill, and was blooded by the Master. How could I, after that, ever forget the *Fox and Duck?*"

Christina laughed.

"The man who kept it then is still there, but he is very old. I know he will be thrilled to see you."

That was an understatement.

In fact, the Innkeeper could hardly believe his eyes when the Marquis walked in.

Having shaken his hand warmly, the Marquis told him what was required, and the whole Inn was in a turmoil.

Christina suggested they should eat outside.

The big wooden table at which the elders of the village drank their ale in the evening was covered with a cloth.

The Proprietor's wife and their pretty, young granddaughter waited on them.

There was no more than bread and cheese, which was all most people expected at the *Fox and Duck* at Luncheontime.

But because Christina and the Marquis were both hungry, everything they were offered seemed delicious.

They did not spend too much time over luncheon, but went on to yet another Farm.

This was on the outskirts of the Estate, which the Marquis could remember from his hunting days as a boy.

It was after five o'clock when they got back and, as they rode up the drive, the Marquis asked:

"Are you very tired? I feel I have behaved somewhat brutally in taking you so far."

"I am not tired, but I suspect I shall be stiff," Christina answered. "It is a long time since I have ridden such a fine horse. In fact, after your Father died, I was soon reduced to the animals in the stable that were left. Then because Papa disapproved so much of Mr. Waters, there was only poor old Ben."

"I am sure Mrs. Dartford can give you something for your stiffness," the Marquis said. "She used to have remedies for everything, and I cannot believe she has not improved on them in the ensuing years."

"She has certainly kept the Herb Garden going," Christina remarked, "and I think she would be very thrilled if you would go and admire it."

"You should have told me about it before," the Marquis said. "How can I know these things if you do not tell me about them?"

"I . . . I am doing . . . my best," Christina said humbly.

"I am only teasing you," the Marquis said as he laughed. "You are proving invaluable to me, and I am very, very grateful."

He spoke with a sincerity in his voice that made Christina blush.

Then she told herself that he would have been just as grateful to her Father.

Or, for that matter, to anyone else, if she had not been there.

As they walked into the hall, Terence Verley came out from the Study.

"So you are back!" he remarked. "I wondered what had happened to you."

"We had to visit the Farms to-day," the Marquis said. "It took so long that we could not get back here for Luncheon."

"That is a pity, because you missed a good meal," Terence said.

There was a slight thickness in his voice which made the Marquis aware that he had not only eaten well, but also imbibed a great deal of wine.

Christina was already half-way up the stairs.

"I am going to change, and also see Miss Dickson," she said to the Marquis as if he had asked her where she was going.

"Give her my love and tell her I will come and see her later," the Marquis said.

"She will enjoy that," Christina replied.

She found Miss Dickson, as she expected, in the *Boudoir* which led off her bedroom.

She had her feet resting comfortably on a sofa, a rug over her legs, and was reading a book.

Christina apologised that they had not been back for Luncheon, and she said:

"Do not worry, dear child, I listened to Mr. Verley being extremely rude about his relatives. If it gave him any pleasure to get it off his chest, then it was better that I should endure it rather than His Lordship!"

"I did not like him when I met him last night," Christina said, "and I have a feeling that he is imposing on the Marquis."

"You can be sure of that," Miss Dickson agreed. "In fact, Mr. Verley has come here in order to extract money from him, and he means to stay until he gets it."

Christina sighed.

"I thought it must be something like that and His Lordship needs all the money he has for the Farmers, besides what has to be done in the villages."

"I know, dear," Miss Dickson said, "and if you ask me, I think Mr. Verley is a 'pain in the neck.' But I do not see how we are to be rid of him."

Christina laughed.

"I love you for saying 'we,' Miss Dickson," she said. "That is something we ought to do."

"I cannot think how," Miss Dickson said. "At the same time, that kind young man should not be bothered when he has so many other problems to solve."

"Have you ever heard of his Cousin Terence before?" Christina enquired.

"I have indeed!" Miss Dickson confirmed. "I remember the old Marquis being furiously angry whenever his Father's name was mentioned, and the servants have told me how his name was erased from the Family Tree."

Christina, when she went down to dinner, thought there was every reason for the Marquis to be annoyed at his Cousin's unexpected appearance.

Terence had obviously been drinking a great deal during the day.

He was not drunk, but somewhat aggressive.

He completely monopolised the conversation at dinner.

He talked about London, his friends there, and the gambling that took place in the Clubs to which he belonged.

He then talked about the huge bets that were placed on the Mills, as the boxing matches were known, which took place outside the City.

It was quite obvious that he had lost a lot of money, both on the fights and on the race-courses, besides, Christina suspected, betting heavily at cards.

When dinner was over, Miss Dickson said she wished to retire for the night.

The Marquis escorted her to the bottom of the stairs.

"You must forgive me for going to bed so early," she said.

"I think you are very wise," the Marquis said, "and as I have so much to do, that is what I intend to do myself."

"I am sure Christina will do the same," Miss Dickson said. "She has had a long

112

day, although she tells me it was a very enjoyable one."

"She is helping me enormously," the Marquis replied. "I am very grateful to you both."

"I am so glad that you are back," Miss Dickson remarked, "that I feel half the age I was yesterday!"

The Marquis laughed.

"I will have you dancing before I have finished," he said.

"That will be the day!" Miss Dickson replied.

The Marquis kissed her good-night.

He thought she walked up the stairs far more easily and sprightly than she had been able to do before.

"Christina is right," he told himself. "What she wants is feeding up, and the comfort of being here. That is why she is going to stay at Melverly until she dies!"

He thought as he walked back to the Drawing-Room that he would arrange a Suite for Miss Dickson so that she could have all her own things around her.

She would be waited on and have every possible comfort.

It struck him that perhaps one day

she would teach his sons as she had taught him.

It was an idea, but he brushed it aside.

"I have no intention of marrying," he told himself.

Then, as he reached the Drawing-Room door, he remembered who was inside.

"Dammit all," he swore to himself. "If that is my Heir Presumptive, I must have a son as quickly as possible!"

As neither the Marquis nor Christina wished to listen to Terence, who continued to be exceedingly voluble, they soon retired to bed.

Nanny helped her undress.

When she had left her, Christina thought how much more delightful it would have been if she and the Marquis could have dined alone.

'His tiresome Cousin is spoiling everything!' she thought.

Then she remembered how much they had done and how happy they had made so many people.

She said a prayer of gratitude knowing that only God could have brought the Marquis home so safely.

'I am grateful . . . very . . . very . . .

grateful,' she thought.

She wished she could say so in Church.

She suddenly remembered that a secret passage in this part of the house led to a small consecrated Chapel.

It had been used first by the Jesuits, who were hiding from the persecution of Queen Elizabeth's men.

Later, it had been re-consecrated for the Royalists, who hid from the Roundheads in Melverley Hall.

There was a Private Chaplain who performed the Service of Communion weekly for everyone in the House.

It was, however, impossible for them to all get into the small Chapel.

They therefore used to go in two at a time, with somebody keeping watch in the hall while they did so.

There was always the possibility of a troop of Roundheads suddenly appearing in the drive.

One Verley who was on Cromwell's *"Wanted"* List had remained undetected and undiscovered for over five years.

He had been hidden all that time at Melverley.

Only when King Charles II came back to England was he free to come out of hiding.

Now Christina thought it would be the right place to go to give thanks for the safe homecoming of the Marquis.

Ever since she had been a small child she had played in the secret passages.

She had been shown them by the Marquis's Father, who had been very fond of her.

She got out of bed and pressed a knot on a panel near the mantel-piece.

It opened.

Picking up one of the candles beside her bed, Christina stepped into the darkness behind it.

She knew the way and did not even stop to put on her dressing-gown.

The passage smelled of old wood, yet it was not damp.

There were occasional flickers of moon-light which came from under the eaves.

Christina moved quickly because she knew the way so well.

She had almost reached the Chapel, when she heard someone speaking.

She stopped instinctively, shading the candle with her hand.

Then she recognised the voice.

It was Terence Verley's.

She was just about to walk on, when she heard him say:

"You have brought the drug with you?"

" 'Course Oi' 'ave, Sir."

She knew it must be the Valet who replied, because the servants had told her he had a Cockney accent.

"And you think the man will co-operate?"

"Oi speaks t'im this mornin' an' tells 'im wot yer'll pay 'im," the Valet replied. " 'E's not bin in 'Is Lordship's employment fer long an' from all Oi 'ears, 'e's a bit soft in the 'ead!"

"But you think he will do what we want?" Terence demanded.

" 'E'll do it, Sir. Oi've promised 'im five pound, an' 'is eyes lit up like a beacon!" the Valet answered.

"Very well," Terence said. "Go and fetch him."

Christina drew in her breath.

She walked on, moving slowly now and far more carefully than she had before.

She passed the Chapel and instead went on to the end of the passage.

She realised that what she heard meant that Terence Verley was intending to do something that would definitely hurt the Marquis.

"I have to save him . . . I have to!" she said to herself.

chapter five

The Marquis had got into bed.

Then he decided that before he went to sleep he would make a list of the things he had promised the Farmers during the day.

He was afraid that when morning came he would have forgotten which Farm required what.

He, therefore, in his strong, upright writing, made some notes on a pad which always stood beside his bed.

He was just checking that what he had promised the first Farm was correct, when he glanced up.

He was then startled into immobility.

A woman in white was standing in a dark part of the room, where the light from the candles did not reach.

It swept through his mind that this must be the "White Lady," the ghost of the Countess Sylvia.

He thought he must be dreaming, but she was definitely there, silhouetted against the panelling.

She stood still until, with an astonished note in his voice, he exclaimed:

"Christina!"

She then moved quickly towards him with her finger to her lips.

As she reached the bed, she said in a whisper he could hardly hear:

"Come . . . quickly! Come . . . with me! It is . . . important!"

She did not wait for the Marquis to answer, but moved back the way she had come.

She stepped through the panelled door, which was open, beside the fireplace.

The Marquis had learnt to be swift and not to procrastinate when anything important occurred.

He leapt out of bed and picked up his robe, which Yates had left on a chair.

He had slipped into it by the time he reached the open panel.

Christina was inside, and now she was holding a candle in her hands.

She did not speak to him, but merely started to move along the secret passage.

The Marquis had played in these passages as a child, but he had almost forgotten his way.

Now he was recalling the thrill it had given him when he had first been shown them by his Father.

He wondered what had upset Christina and what was happening.

Then, as she stopped and put the candle down on the floor, he heard a voice.

He was aware it came from the room in which his Cousin Terence was sleeping.

Then he heard him say:

"Good-evening! My Valet tells me that you are prepared to do something for me which I think will amuse His Lordship."

"Yes, Sir," a man replied.

Now Christina moved a tiny shutter in the wall.

The Marquis remembered that he would be able to see through it into the bedroom.

He could look through it only with one eye.

But it was enough for him to see that his Cousin Terence was sitting on the bed.

Standing in front of him was the man he had seen at the door of his room whom he knew was his Valet.

There was also another man wearing the white coat and apron of a Chef.

The Marquis guessed, although he did

not think he had seen the man before, that he was an assistant to the Chef he had brought with him from London.

He suspected it was the young man who had been walking with his Chef towards the Kitchen when he had spoken to him about Mrs. Boswin, the Cook.

"Now, what I have planned," he heard Terence saying, "is a joke on my Cousin, the Marquis. It is something which you add to the food and which, when he eats it, makes a man laugh heartily even if he is depressed or hears bad news."

Terence paused and looked at the young man.

He was thinking to himself that there was a somewhat vacant expression on his face.

"Do you understand what I am saying?" he asked.

"I — I thinks so, — Sir."

"Then what you have to do," Terence went on, "is to add it to the *soufflé* which I intend to ask for as a special dish at the end of dinner to-morrow night. Is that clear?"

The young man nodded.

"Mix it carefully so that no-one will

suspect anything until His Lordship starts laughing."

There was no response.

Terence brought something from his pocket.

"Here is a sovereign in advance," he said, "and you shall have another nine when you have put what is in this small bottle into the *soufflé*."

The Marquis saw him hand the bottle to the Assistant Chef, who looked at it curiously.

"And, of course," Terence went on, "as it is to be a joke, you must tell no-one — absolutely no-one — otherwise they may warn His Lordship and he will not eat the dish."

"In which case," the Valet warned, "you'll get nothin'."

"I'll do as you say, Sir," the Assistant Chef murmured.

"Thank you. I know it is something that will amuse His Lordship," Terence said.

The Valet opened the door for the Assistant Chef and he went from the room.

Neither Terence nor his Valet spoke until they were quite certain the Assistant Chef was out of hearing.

Then Terence Verley said reflectively:

"It should work just as we are drinking port and there are no servants in the room."

"Then 'E'll do wot you tell 'im," Wills said.

"I will have both cheques ready," Terence went on as if he had not heard what his Valet had said, "and as soon as he has signed them you will leave for London immediately. You are certain that stable lad you spoke to will take you?"

" 'E finks we're goin' to a bull fight wot 'e 'ticularly wants ter see, and 'e'll be back afore breakfast. 'E's in fer a nasty surprise when we reaches London," the Valet replied.

"I am only afraid," Terence said, "that someone will talk."

"Oi doubts it, Sir," the Valet answered. "Them as wants money c'n allus manage ter keep their moufs shut!"

"That is true," Terence Verley agreed. "Now let me go to bed, and for God's sake give me another glass of that wine you brought upstairs for me. I am worn out with all this plotting and planning!"

The man had obviously anticipated what his Master required.

He was already pouring some rich red

wine into a large glass.

Christina reached up and shut the peephole through which the Marquis had been watching.

As if he knew what she wanted, he walked slowly and very quietly back to his bedroom.

As he stepped inside, Christina followed him.

She was in the shadows by the door in the panelling.

But the Marquis was aware that he could see the outline of her exquisite body through the material of her night-gown.

Quite unselfconsciously, Christina asked:

"You . . . realise what he . . . intends to . . . do?"

"Of course I do," the Marquis answered, "and I have heard of that drug. It completely numbs the brain so that the victim does exactly as he is told without question, and without being able to think."

Christina, despite herself, gave a little cry.

"You must be careful . . . very careful!"

"You have saved me a lot of money, and my self-respect," the Marquis said.

"I will turn Terence out of the house to-morrow morning, and if he goes to prison, or starves, I will not raise a finger to help him!"

He spoke quietly. At the same time, Christina knew how angry he was.

Instinctively she put her hand on his arm.

"Please . . . be careful . . . be very careful," she said again. "I do not . . . trust him. If he cannot obtain the money by this means, he will try another."

The Marquis did not speak, and she said:

"Papa always said that . . . a cornered rat is dangerous. I think you would be wiser . . . to postpone giving him a . . . definite answer, and not antagonise him."

Unexpectedly the Marquis smiled.

"You look at the moment like a small child," he said. "Yet you have an extremely astute brain and you are as wise as my Mother would have been where I am concerned."

"Then . . . you will . . . do as I . . . suggest?" Christina asked.

"Because you have saved me from giving that young swine money which should be spent on the Estate, I will think of another way of getting rid of him, but it will not be easy."

"I know he is dangerous," Christina said. "If anything . . . happened to you, can you imagine what it would mean to all the people who live here, and your . . . family, who depend . . . on you?"

The Marquis knew she was talking sense.

"Go to bed, Christina," he said. "I do not need to tell you that you have been wonderful! I will think of some way of removing my Cousin Terence from Melverley, if nothing else!"

Christina smiled.

Then, as she stepped inside the open panel, the Marquis asked:

"Incidentally, what were you doing in the secret passage at this time of night?"

"I was on my way to the Chapel," Christina answered, "to thank God for all . . . you have . . . done to-day, and for the . . . happiness . . . you have . . . brought to the Farmers."

The Marquis smiled.

"So that was the reason," he said. "I thought when I first saw you standing there that you were the 'White Lady' come to warn me of danger."

"If I was," Christina answered, "then you must be the 'Black knight' who saves yourself and everybody else from . . . your Cousin."

As she finished speaking, she pulled the panel door to very quietly.

The Marquis found himself alone in his room.

He could hardly believe that what had just happened could be true.

And yet he supposed it was something he might have expected of his disreputable Cousin.

Terence was obviously desperate for money.

"I must think what to do," he told himself as he got back into bed.

As he blew out the candles he thought of Christina praying in the secret Chapel, which, of course, he remembered.

She was right in going there, because only prayer could be of assistance in a situation like this.

Christina came down to breakfast the following morning, feeling very apprehensive.

She had prayed for a long time in the Chapel.

She was sure the Marquis would find a way of getting rid of his Cousin without making him angry, in which case he would find another way of obtaining the money he required.

She thought how frightening it was that only the Marquis stood between Terence and the title.

With it went the huge fortune which the Head of the Family administered.

She was quite certain that if Terence became the fifth Marquis, none of the money would be given to the Farmers or the Pensioners.

The Estate would become even more run down than it was at the moment.

"Oh . . . please . . . God, help us find a way of getting . . . rid of him!" she prayed as she dressed.

When she found the Marquis in the Breakfast-Room, she felt irrepressible joy in her heart because he was still alive.

As he knew it was what she wanted to hear, the Marquis said:

"I have found a way of carrying out your instructions."

"Y-you . . . have?" Christina murmured. "Please . . . tell me . . . what it . . . is."

The Marquis sat down at the head of the table and poured himself a cup of coffee.

Christina realised he wished her to help herself to something to eat before they discussed what he had in mind.

She hastily took the lid off the first *entrée* dish she came to and put a small amount of scrambled egg onto a plate.

As she sat down at the table, the Marquis said:

"You were right to warn me last night, and it would be a mistake to antagonise my Cousin until he has nothing to lose by attempting to kill me."

Christina drew in her breath.

"It seems a . . . terrible thing to say, but I feel he . . . might do that . . . if you refuse to . . . help him."

"I find it difficult to think that a member of my family could stoop to murder," the Marquis said, "but because it is a possibility, I have decided to give him two thousand pounds and send him back to London."

Christina made a little sound but did not interrupt.

"I will promise him that, when I, too, return to London, which will be in the near future," the Marquis went on, "I will discuss with my Solicitors the possibility of making him an allowance which he will receive monthly — of course on the condition that he does not exceed it."

"And . . . and you will pay his debts?" Christina asked.

The Marquis made a gesture with his hands.

"I suppose I have no alternative," he answered. "But it is something which I must somehow make certain does not occur again."

"I hope . . . you will be . . . able to do . . . that," Christina said, "but I do not . . . think it is . . . going to be . . . easy."

Her words were prophetic.

When at noon the Marquis came back with Christina, after they had been riding, Terence had only just come downstairs.

Christina disappeared, and the Marquis took him into the Study.

He told him what he had arranged and knew at once that Terence was disappointed.

He was thinking of what he had planned for the evening and was determined not to leave the Hall.

The Marquis, however, was firm.

"I am sending you back to London to-day, immediately after Luncheon," he said, "because it is important that you should get together all your accounts so that we can show them to the Solicitors as soon as I arrive."

"And when will that be?" Terence asked.

"As soon as I have finished what I have to do here," the Marquis replied. "Unfortunately the Estate Manager whom my Father trusted has proved to be a crook and a thief and I therefore have to put things to rights before I can return to London."

"Then I think I should stay here with you," Terence said.

"As I have already explained," the Marquis said, "you have a great deal to do so as to be ready the minute I arrive. Quite frankly, Terence, you will understand that at the moment I have no time for entertaining anyone, but must concentrate on the people who have been shamefully neglected while I have been in France."

That at least was the truth, and Terence somewhat reluctantly said:

"Very well, I will go to London, if you

insist, but two thousand pounds will not go very far."

"Give a small amount to each of the Tradesmen to whom you owe money," the Marquis said, "with the promise that their total bills will be met as soon as possible."

"I doubt if they will believe me," Terence said with a twist of his lips.

"I am sure you can persuade them," the Marquis replied.

Just for a moment he thought that Terence was going to defy him and insist he had to have more, or remain at Melverley.

Then, to the Marquis's surprise, he said:

"Very well, I will do as you say, but I hope you are sending me to London in comfort."

"I am afraid there is only the Travelling Carriage with two horses," the Marquis said, "as I shall need the team with which to return myself. But as there is a change of horses waiting for you on the way, you should reach London before midnight."

Because he had no wish to go on arguing, he walked to his desk and picked up an envelope.

"There is five hundred pounds in notes here," he said, "and a cheque for fifteen hundred. Do not forget to leave me your address so that I can get in touch with you on my arrival."

Somewhat grudgingly, Terence wrote it down, saying:

"It is the address of a friend, as you will see, but if it is not convenient for me to stay there, I will move into your house in Berkeley Square."

It was a threat, and the Marquis knew it.

Almost as if Christina had put a finger against his lips, he did not say what came into his mind.

It was that if Terence attempted to move into the house in Berkeley Square, he would instruct his servants not to admit him.

Luncheon was served at twelve-thirty.

At one o'clock Terence and his Valet were driving away from Melverley Hall.

Only when the Travelling Carriage was out of sight did Christina say:

"They have gone, and I can only pray that they will . . . not come . . . back."

"Amen to that!" the Marquis said. "But I have a feeling we are being optimistic. However, at least now we are free to get on with the work we are doing."

The Marquis decided his first visit should be to the Alms Houses, which had been built by his Father.

They contained twelve Pensioners, men and women too old to look after themselves in a cottage of their own.

Christina thought it was decidedly more comfortable for them than the dilapidated cottages in the village.

At the same time, there was a lot to be done to the Alms Houses themselves.

The Warden told the Marquis that they had been so short of money that, on several days in the week, the old people had gone hungry.

After the Alms Houses, they inspected the Schools.

These the Marquis learnt, to his fury, had not been kept up during the war.

The Teachers had been dismissed.

Because the Schools were situated at the opposite end of the Estate, Christina had not been aware of what had occurred.

The Marquis made a note that they had to find Teachers.

In one village they were lucky enough to meet a retired School Master who promised to get the School started again.

He said he would supervise it until new Teachers could be found to take his place.

By the time they returned to the Hall, they had covered a great number of miles.

Christina was obviously tired.

"I am making you do too much," the Marquis said, "and I apologise."

"It is not that we have done too much this afternoon," Christina answered, "but I was worried this morning that Mr. Verley would not leave. His being in the house frightened me, and I kept wondering all the time what he would do next."

"Well, he should be in London by this time," the Marquis said soothingly.

Christina, however, was thinking that if she had not decided to go to the Priest's Chapel last night, the Marquis would have eaten the *soufflé* at dinner.

Then he would have become completely subservient to his Cousin because of the drug it contained.

The Marquis sent for the Assistant Chef.

He told him he had discovered the trick that was to be played on him and that he was part and parcel of it.

"If you ever do such a thing again," he said sternly, "you will be dismissed without a reference."

The Assistant Chef almost wept as he apologised abjectly.

The Marquis accepted his apology.

He said he would not dismiss him this time, but give him a second chance.

The man then took the sovereign from his pocket and, putting it on the Marquis's desk, said:

"I knows I done wrong, M'Lord, an' I won' do nothin' like it again."

"Mind that you do not," the Marquis said. "And what I suggest you do now is to put this sovereign in the Offertory Box in the Church which you will find at the end of the Park. I trust you to do that."

The Assistant Chef swore that he would, and the Marquis sent him back to the Kitchen.

The Marquis gave a sigh of relief when he sat down to dinner, having learnt that Miss Dickson was not going to join them.

She had sent a message to say that she hoped the Marquis would understand, but she had a headache and had gone to bed.

"Is she really ill?" he asked Christina when she joined him.

Her eyes twinkled.

"I think, if you want the truth," she said, "Miss Dickson is being tactful. She is astute enough to realise that something has upset us. She does not know what it is, but she has loved you ever since you were a little boy, and she always knew when something was wrong."

"I am sure that is true," the Marquis agreed.

"She said to me," Christina went on, " 'If you two young people have a problem, you do not want me there, and Mrs. Dartford has promised me a delicious dinner with, believe it or not, a glass of champagne!' "

Christina smiled as she remembered that she replied:

"You are wonderful, Miss Dickson, as you have always been!"

The Marquis thought it was very like Dickie to be so understanding.

She guessed he would want to talk to Christina about the things that concerned them both.

He remembered how bored he had been last night with Terence droning on about himself.

They did not stay long in the Drawing-Room after dinner.

Christina said she wanted to go to bed, and would say good-night to Miss Dickson on the way.

"Give her a kiss from me," the Marquis said, "and, as we have a lot to do to-morrow, I will order the horses to be round at nine o'clock."

"I shall be looking forward to that," Christina answered.

She walked towards the door and, as the Marquis opened it for her, she said:

"I will not go to the Priest's Chapel to-night, but I will thank God that you sent Mr. Verley away, and you need not be . . . afraid of . . . everything you . . . eat or drink."

The Marquis was aware that it was still worrying her, and he said:

"Forget it! It is something he will not do again."

Because he was so touched by Christina's concern, he took her hand in his and lifted it to his lips.

"I do not know what I should do without you, Christina," he said.

He saw her eyes shine, and a touch of colour came into her cheeks.

He shut the door behind her.

Then he told himself he must be careful not to let her fall in love with him.

'She is very young,' he thought, 'and, apart from the ghastly Sir Mortimer, I do not suppose she has met many men.'

It would be a crime for him to go back to London and leave her with a broken heart.

Then he knew that she thought of him more as a Father figure and he was worrying needlessly.

She would doubtless expect a Suitor to be young, perhaps, at the most, twenty-two years of age.

'I am getting old,' the Marquis said to himself.

It suddenly occurred to him that that was the truth.

It was time he settled down and had an heir.

That, he thought, would put paid to Terence's position as his Heir Presumptive.

Christina, having said good-night to Miss Dickson, went to her own bedroom.

She realised how tired she was.

Despite Mrs. Dartford's excellent herbal remedy to prevent stiffness, she was finding it painful to move quickly.

It had been so long since she had been without a mount.

'I will be all right in the morning,' she told herself.

Because she was used to looking after herself, she had told Nanny not to wait up for her.

She could not ask one of the house-maids either, without hurting the old Nurse's feelings.

Nanny was delighted to be at the Hall.

She was enjoying the good food and having nothing to do except wash and press Christina's clothes.

"I hope everything is all right at home," Christina had said that morning.

"I'm not worryin' about that at the moment," Nanny replied. "I'm just enjoying meself, and that's what you ought to be doing too, Dearie. We've put up with enough discomfort these past years."

Christina thought it had not only been uncomfortable during her Father's illness, but also that they had had so many worries.

The Marquis had swept these away for the moment.

She did not have to worry now about the future.

She was just getting into bed, when

she went to the window to have a last look at the stars.

It was something she had always done at home.

Now the stars seemed somehow brighter and the moon more silvery than it had been before.

The window was open, and as she looked out she heard a strange sound.

She thought at first it was the cry of a bird.

Then, as it came again and again, she realised it was the miaow of a cat in pain.

There were several cats about the place, and she thought one might have been caught in a trap.

The cry was repeated.

Although she leaned further out of the window, she could not make out where the sound was coming from.

She wondered if she could call the Marquis for help.

Then she thought that doubtless he would be asleep.

If she was tired, he was tired too.

She put on her dressing-gown, a pretty one made of blue flannel, which Nanny had made for her.

It fastened down the front with small pearl buttons.

She went again to the window to make certain the cat was still miaowing.

It was.

'I am sure it is caught in something,' she thought, 'and if it is not a trap, it might be some wire-netting.'

She opened the door of her room to find that the candles in the sconces had been extinguished with the exception of two.

Running down the stairs, she decided to ask the Night Porter to come with her.

When she got there, however, she found that he was fast asleep.

He was in the curved, padded chair which was always used by the footman on duty.

He was a young lad from the village.

Christina knew he had not been properly fed during the last years of the war.

He was therefore very thin and pale.

She knew, however, he would soon be better with three good meals a day.

She was reluctant to disturb him.

Instead, she walked quietly to the front-door and slipped back the bolts.

Then she turned the key which was so well oiled that it made no sound.

She ran down the stone steps and

heard the cry come again.

She thought it was from a big bush on the other side of the court-yard.

As she went, walking in her bedroom slippers over the gravel, she heard the same sound again.

It was very dark, and the moonlight did not reach one side of the bushes.

At first Christina stood still, then she took a step forward, her hand outstretched in front of her.

Suddenly a heavy cloth was flung over her head.

She gave a cry of fear, but her voice was lost in the thickness of the material.

She felt herself being lifted up, obviously by a man.

She tried to struggle, but the cloth that covered her made it impossible.

She could not move her arms, but, as she tried to kick, she felt her feet being tied together.

She screamed, but her voice was muffled.

Then, as the man carrying her began to move, she knew without being told that it was Terence Verley.

chapter six

Christina was being carried over rough ground.

Then, so suddenly that she gave a shriek, she was thrown down.

Only as a horse started off and she was moving did she realise she had been put into a cart.

Not only was there a rope securing her feet, there was also one round her arms over the rug, so that she could not move them.

The cart was an open one, she thought, such as the gardeners used.

One horse was pulling it, and he moved very quickly.

It was agony as she was thrown from side to side and her head hit the wood beneath it.

She knew it was Terence who had spirited her away, but she could not imagine where he was taking her, or why.

She realised that no-one would know why she had left the house.

The Night Porter, however, might think it strange that the door was open.

It would be Nanny, when she went to

call her, who would be aware that her bed had not been slept in and raise the alarm.

'Why is he . . . doing this? Where is he . . . taking me?' she wondered.

They were moving along what she guessed was just a cart-track.

Then they were bumping along over rough, uncultivated ground.

It seemed to her she had been travelling for a long time.

It was difficult to breathe because of the thickness of the rug over her face.

At last the cart came to a standstill.

For the first time, the man who was driving it made a sound.

It was a shrill whistle, and a moment later there was the sound of footsteps coming towards them.

"I have got her, Wills!" Terence Verley said, and there was no mistaking his voice.

"Everythin's ready fer yer up at t'top, but watch it as 'em stairs be creakin'," Wills replied.

"I will be careful," Terence Verley answered.

Christina felt herself being dragged from the cart into his arms.

She was thrown over his shoulder in

a "Fireman's Lift," and it was impossible for her to struggle.

In any case, she had no wish to, in case he should drop her.

Now he was walking over some gravel, and then it was as if he went in through a door.

After that there were steps. Wills was right in saying they were creaking.

Christina was afraid they might give way under such a heavy load.

Up, up, up Terence carried her.

Then he was walking across a wood floor until he put her roughly down onto the ground.

Christina waited.

She was wondering desperately whether he would go away and leave her still imprisoned inside the rug.

To her relief, however, he took the ropes from her body.

As he did so, Christina heard footsteps coming up the stairs they had just climbed.

"Ai've tied up th' 'orse so 'e won't wander away," Wills said.

"Get the rope off her legs," Terence ordered.

The rope had been tied so tightly that it took Wills some time to undo it.

It cut into Christina's ankles as he did so.

As he finished, Terence Verley lifted the rug from her.

For a moment it was difficult to focus her eyes after being in the darkness.

Then she was aware that she was in a small, almost square room.

The only light came from two candles that were on the floor.

Then, as she looked up at Terence Verley's face, she thought he looked as evil as the Devil.

"I hope Your Ladyship is feeling comfortable," he drawled in a mocking tone, "because this is where you are going to stay, and perhaps die, if His Lordship does not come to the rescue."

"Wh-what are you . . . s-saying?" Christina asked. "Why . . . have you . . . brought me . . . here?"

Terence Verley gave an unpleasant laugh.

"I should have thought that was obvious. Naturally the Marquis will want to rescue anything so young, pretty, and attentive as yourself."

Because the way he spoke was so insulting, Christina did not answer.

Wills, who was standing looking down at her, said:

"Come on, Sir. Gimme th' letter. It's gonna tak' me some time t'walk back after Ai've left th' cart."

"Leave it exactly where you found it," Terence ordered. "The letter is ready, except for one thing."

"Wot's that?" Wills enquired.

"I want this pretty bit o' muslin to add her plea to mine," Terence Verley replied. "If I cannot reach the Marquis's heart, hers should do it."

"Tha's a good idea!" Wills conceded.

Terence Verley walked towards one of the candles on the floor.

Christina saw him pick up a piece of paper which lay beside it.

With difficulty, because she felt as if she were still constrained by the ropes, Christina sat up.

She pushed herself back so that she could lean against the wall.

Terence Verley came to her, holding in his hand what was obviously a letter.

"I have written this to His High and Mightiness," he told her, "and you had better read what I have said."

He handed it to Christina.

As if he had given the order, Wills

brought the other candle and put it down beside her.

Because she was frightened, for a moment what was written swam before her eyes.

Then she read:

"My dear Cousin,
I find on thinking it over that your proposition is unacceptable. I have also learnt from my manservant that it is entirely due to that golden-haired chit that you found out about the Estate Manager and are now intending to spend the family fortune on a lot of ignorant, ungrateful countryfolk!

She is obviously determined to marry you, which will certainly ruin my prospects, so I have therefore taken her prisoner. If you require her services in the future, you will have to pay me £500,000 for her. . . ."

Christina gave a gasp of horror, but because there was more, she read on:

"That should provide me with a few comforts which are only my due. Although I may have to ensure that

149

between you you do not produce an heir.

Should you decide that the girl is not worth the price I put on her, she will soon starve to death, as I shall not feed her, and every day that you procrastinate in answering my demands, she will be thrashed insensible.

I think, my dear Cousin, in your guise as a hero, it would be very much wiser for you to pay the price I ask. If you agree, raise a white flag on your mast on top of the Hall. I will then release the girl when the money has been transferred to my Bank — Coutt's — in Lombard Street.

Hoping you will see sense,
I remain,
Your affectionate Cousin,
Terence."

Christina read the note to the end. Then she said furiously:

"How can you . . . ask such . . . a thing? How can you . . . imagine that he would pay . . . so much money . . . for me?"

"Only you can answer those questions," Terence replied. "As I said in the letter, you must blame yourself for being such a 'busy-body' that he has started to spend the Melverley fortune on his damned Estate!"

Christina did not reply, and he went on:

"It is no use denying what you have been up to, and that you see yourself as the Marchioness of Melverley. Wills listened to your Nurse talking in the Housekeeper's Room, and that made me aware of how dangerous you are."

"I am not . . . dangerous," Christina protested. "I was only trying to . . . help the people who have been the . . . responsibility of . . . your family for . . . generations."

"And one far too expensive!" Terence snarled. "If you had left them alone, they would doubtless have died of starvation — as you will!"

He almost spat the words at her.

Then in a different voice he said:

"But of course the Hero will rescue you because there is nothing else he can do. And do not think for a moment he will do it except by paying up. No-one will find you here — no-one!"

It was as he spoke that Christina was suddenly aware of where she was.

There was the "quack" of a duck outside.

She knew, as if he had told her in so many words, that she was in the old Mill.

It was a derelict building which had been abandoned long ago because it was of no further use.

Because it was on a dangerous whirlpool, the land had not been cultivated even before the war.

This was because two sheep had fallen into the whirlpool water and been drowned.

With a sinking of her heart she knew that it would never occur to the Marquis that that was where his Cousin might have hidden her.

He was right when he said that she would never be found.

She would starve to death unless the Marquis paid him the money he was demanding for her release.

As if Terence Verley had read her thoughts, he said:

"You see how clever I have been!"

"You . . . you cannot . . . do this to me . . . you cannot!" Christina cried.

"You will soon find that I shall keep to every word I have put in that letter,"

Terence Verley replied. "It is you who is throwing away on a lot of nincompoops what should be mine, and it is you who are trying to marry my Cousin and give him a son who will steal from me my inheritance."

Now he spoke in a way which made Christina feel he was mad.

He had turned from being an educated man into a snarling animal.

"I will beat you," he was threatening, "for what you have done to me, and enjoy doing it!"

He sounded so violent that Wills stepped forward and put his hand on his arm.

"Cum on, Sir," he pleaded, "we're wastin' time. Gimme th' letter, an' there's a bottle o' good port waitin' for yer below."

"All right," Terence Verley agreed reluctantly. "But I will beat her until she pleads for mercy — as she will do!"

He took a pencil out of his pocket and handed it to Christina.

At the same time, Wills picked up a piece of wood that was lying on the floor.

He put it on Christina's lap for her to write on.

Christina took the pencil and spread out the letter on the wood.

She was trying frantically to think of a way to let the Marquis know where she was.

She might have guessed that Terence Verley would be prepared for this, for he said:

"One word that might be a pointer to where you are hidden, and I will give you a taste of the whip without waiting for to-morrow!"

Desperately, frantically, Christina was praying for help.

Then slowly, writing carefully so that it would not be difficult for the Marquis to read, she wrote:

"I am praying to St. Christopher that you will save me."

She did not sign her name, but just added a capital "C" after what she had written.

Terence Verley snatched the letter from her and read it suspiciously.

"Who is 'St. Christopher'?" he asked.

"My Patron Saint," Christina explained. "If I had been a boy, I would have been baptised Christopher."

Terence Verley snorted because he thought she was talking a lot of rubbish.

He folded the letter and handed it to Wills.

"Hurry up!" he ordered. "I hope you have left me something comfortable on which to sleep downstairs."

"Ai' done me best, Sir," Wills answered, "an' if the rats bites yer toes, don' blame me!"

Christina gave a little cry of horror.

She had forgotten there would be rats in the old Mill.

Wills was already descending the stairs as he spoke.

As Terence Verley was about to follow him, he turned back.

"Until to-morrow, you tiresome little interferer!" he said. "Unless, of course, you would like me to stay and keep you warm?"

There was an unpleasant note in his voice.

Christina turned her face away from him.

He must have been aware of how much she was hating him, for he laughed unpleasantly.

He went down the stairs.

She heard him shutting the door at

the bottom of them and turning the key in the lock.

It was then the fear that had been eating away inside her seemed to well up until she put her hands up to her face.

She did not cry.

She only felt despairingly that the Marquis would not find her, which meant that she would die in this horrible place.

Anyway, how could he possibly pay the enormous sum that Terence Verley was demanding?

She had listened for years to her Father and the old Marquis talking about the Estate.

She was aware that the Melverleys had never sold an acre of land.

Nor had any of its treasures ever been pawned or sold all down the centuries.

Oliver Cromwell had stolen some of them.

The Verleys fighting with Marlborough had run up large debts to provide his men with better food and uniforms than were supplied by the Government.

But the debts had been paid off and the pictures, furniture, and the fertile acres had all remained in the family.

The same thing applied to what they owned in London.

Lord Coventry had gambled away several streets in one night's gaming at Whites Club.

But neither the Earls, nor the Marquises of Melverley, had parted with anything.

Christina knew that to find half-a-million pounds would cripple the family finances as nothing else had ever been able to.

'He must . . . not do it for . . . me! He must . . . not!' she thought.

It was then she thought with horror of what would happen to her if he did not.

It was obvious that Terence Verley was deranged and he would do anything to obtain money.

Even if he obtained it, Christina had a feeling that he would in some way prevent the Marquis from having an heir.

He might kill the present Marquis, or he might wait and kill off any sons that were born to him.

"I could not . . . bear it if that . . . should happen," Christina told herself.

Then, as she thought of the Marquis, so strong, handsome, and so very kind, she knew without realising it that she loved him.

How could she help loving him?

It was a shock.

Yet she knew he had been there in her heart ever since he had helped her the day Ben was killed, then again when Sir Mortimer was pestering her!

After that he had shown inestimable kindness towards the people on his Estate.

She could still picture the Farmer's wife with tears running down her cheeks, and the Farmer himself staring incredulously when the Marquis told him what he was prepared to do.

"He is so wonderful, so magnificent!" Christina said to herself. "And if I die . . . it will be . . . impossible, then, for his wicked Cousin to go on . . . blackmailing him."

She rose to her feet, aware that her ankles hurt from where they had been bound.

She went to the window.

The river beneath the Mill was in darkness.

She looked up to where the stars

were shining in the sky.

The moon she had seen earlier had gone behind a cloud.

Still in the starlight she could see the other side of the river.

There were no houses in sight and the land looked desolate.

It was then she knew that her only chance of survival was if the Marquis understood what she had written.

He must work it out very quickly.

If not, only God could tell him what it meant so that he could find her.

She put her fingers together and looked up at the stars.

By now the Marquis would be asleep.

He would be lying in the great four-poster in which he had been when she had gone to waken him last night.

How would he guess?

How could he imagine for one moment that she had been spirited away?

Why should he question that what he had arranged would not be acceptable?

He had given Terence Verley enough money to keep him in comfort.

Yet, in some crafty manner, he had managed to creep back without anyone being aware of it.

She was helpless in a place from

which she could not escape.

"The Marquis must not give all that money for me!" she said, looking up at the stars. "Please, God, let him understand what I have written and know where I am. Perhaps by a miracle You could think of a means by which I could escape?"

Even as she prayed she thought it was hopeless.

Yet because her mother had said that "Good always triumphs over evil," she could not believe there was not an answer.

The Marquis must find it.

"He is so strong, so intelligent," she told herself.

She felt her love for him surging up from within her heart.

"I love . . . him! I love . . . him!" she admitted.

As she looked up at the stars, it seemed as if they repeated the words as they glistened and glimmered in the dark sky.

Finally she turned from the window.

She realised then that the candles were flickering and would not last very long.

There was nothing to lie on except for

the thick rug with which she had been covered.

Terence Verley had left it on the floor.

She lay down, turning a corner of it so as to make a pillow for her head.

The candles burnt lower.

She looked about her apprehensively, afraid the rats might come near her when it was dark.

Then she told herself sensibly that the Mill had not been in use for many years.

Anything edible would have been devoured by the rats a long time ago.

'If only the Marquis were here . . . he would . . . frighten them . . . away,' she thought.

Only to think of him made little thrills run through her body.

"How can I have . . . loved him all this time without . . . realising it?" she asked herself.

Then she knew that she had never loved anyone with the same feelings that she had for him.

It was what she knew her Father had felt for her Mother.

It was why they had been so happy all the years they had been together.

It was exactly what she wanted to find herself, also she knew it was why she had been repulsed by Sir Mortimer Stinger when he approached her.

Then she remembered how important the Marquis was and that he must have known many women who had loved him, women he had loved in return.

'He will never think of me except as someone who helped him when he came home to such chaos,' she thought unhappily, 'but I shall love him all my life and there will never be another man to compare with him in any way.'

Then the terror of the predicament she was in swept over her.

The thought of what might happen to-morrow made her clench her fingers together.

Once again she was praying.

"Please, God . . . please . . . let him . . . s-save me . . . !"

The Marquis awoke early, as he always did.

He lay, expecting Yates to call him, when there was a knock on the door.

Without stopping to think, he called, "Come in!"

To his surprise, Christina's Nanny appeared.

"Oh, M'Lord, excuse me!" she said,

dropping him a curtsy. "But Miss Christina's not in her room!"

The Marquis sat up in bed.

"Not in her room? What do you mean? Where is she?" the Marquis asked.

"Her bed's not bin slept in, M'Lord, an' she's nowhere to be found!" answered Christina's Nanny.

The Marquis stared at her in astonishment.

"Is that possible?"

"Come an' see for yourself, M'Lord, an' Henry, who was on duty last night, says the front-door was unlocked this morning!" Nanny exclaimed.

The Marquis was silent for a moment. Then he said:

"There is obviously something wrong! I will get up as quickly as possible, Nanny."

"I don't know what's happening, that I don't," Nanny said tearfully, "but my baby must be — somewhere!"

The Marquis got out of bed and rang the bell for Yates, who came hurrying in.

"I knows as 'ow you'd be wantin' me, Yer Lordship," he said. "I've jes' bin told by 'Enry. The door 'e was supposed to be guardin' was ajar when 'e wakes up this mornin'."

The Marquis did not answer.

He was dressing as fast as he could.

Five minutes later he was downstairs, having looked into Christina's bedroom.

He saw, as Nanny had said, that the bed had not been slept in.

Nanny also informed him that Christina's dressing-gown and bedroom slippers were missing too.

As he reached the hall, Johnson came hurrying towards him.

"I've been making enquiries of everyone in the Kitchen, M'Lord," he said before the Marquis could speak. "No-one can throw any light on what's happened to Miss Christina. But this note was found pushed under the back door."

He handed the Marquis the note on a silver salver.

As the Marquis took it, he recognised Terence's hand-writing.

Carrying it to his Study, he shut the door behind him before opening the note.

He read it, and for a moment was too furious to move.

He read the letter twice, thinking he must be mistaken.

No Gentleman could sink so low or be so utterly vile as to make threats.

Then he told himself that he was

dealing with a madman.

There was therefore no point in getting angry.

He had to use his brain if he was to defeat Terence and rescue Christina.

He read what she had written again and again.

He did not understand why she had included St. Christopher in her plea for help.

He could understand the horror and terror she must have been feeling when she wrote her message.

He felt he could have killed Terence with his bare hands for torturing her in such a way.

He was still studying the letter, when Johnson came into the room.

"I thought Your Lordship should know that the Travelling Chariot in which Mr. Terence left here," he said, "has returned."

"Returned?" the Marquis questioned.

"Yes, M'Lord. The driver says that Mr. Terence made him stop at the first Posting-Inn on the main highway. He then told him to wait until the morning to come back to Melverley."

"Mr. Terence did not come back with him?" the Marquis enquired.

"No, M'Lord, and when the driver made enquiries at the Posting-Inn, he learnt that Mr. Terence had taken a Post Chaise back here."

The Marquis's lips tightened, but he did not say anything.

"And there's something else," Johnson went on. "I thought I ought to tell Your Lordship, although it may have nothing to do with Miss Christina's disappearance."

"What is it?" the Marquis asked.

"One of the garden boys came into the Kitchen to say that someone took the horse that draws the vegetable cart out of his stall last night."

"How does he know that?" the Marquis asked sharply.

"Well, Your Lordship, he stables the horse himself, but this morning some of the harness was still on him. He also says the cart has been moved from where he left it."

The Marquis considered this.

It told him two things — Christina was somewhere in the vicinity.

She had been taken on the vegetable cart to some hiding place, where Terence was keeping her prisoner.

If he was able to see the white flag

flying from the roof, then he could not be very far away.

Obviously Christina was with him.

'If I have to pull up every blade of grass and cut down every tree, I will find her!' the Marquis vowed to himself.

It was then he looked once again at the note in his hand, and had an idea.

chapter seven

Carrying the letter from Terence, the Marquis ran upstairs.

He went into the *Boudoir* which adjoined Miss Dickson's bedroom and found her there, as he had expected.

Nanny was with her, still wiping the tears from her eyes.

"Do not get up," the Marquis said as he entered, knowing they were both about to rise. "I want to ask you, Dickie, what you know about St. Christopher."

She smiled at him.

"I taught you all about him a long time ago," she answered.

"He is the Patron Saint of Travellers and was martyred for being a Christian."

She looked at the Marquis to see what more he required, and after a moment she went on:

"The legends, which I am sure I told you, represented him as a giant who devoted his life to carrying travellers across a river."

"A river!" the Marquis exclaimed.

He looked down again at the letter.

"That is what Christina must be trying

to tell me," he said. "She is somewhere near a river."

He was speaking half to himself, but Nanny gave a shrill cry.

"That's where that devil's hidden her! I knows where she is! She's in the old Mill!"

Both the Marquis and Miss Dickson turned to look at Nanny in astonishment.

Then Miss Dickson said:

"It is certainly a possibility. No-one would think of looking for her there!"

"The Mill? What Mill?" the Marquis asked sharply.

"It's the Mill that was used years ago when I first came to the village," Nanny began.

"And I remember your Father," Miss Dickson interposed, "having it fenced off because sheep had fallen into the whirlpool."

The Marquis glanced down again at the letter in his hand.

Then he said:

"Christina says, 'I am praying to St. Christopher to save me.'"

"Then that is what she is telling you," Miss Dickson said.

"Now that I think of it, I remember where that old Mill is," the Marquis

169

went on. "It is at the end of a field on which I was not allowed to ride. Now I know what to do!"

He went towards the door, and Nanny cried out:

"Save her — Your Lordship! Save her! I can't bear to think what's — happenin' to my — poor baby!"

The Marquis was gone and Miss Dickson said soothingly:

"Leave it in His Lordship's hands. I know that he will not fail us, and all we can do, Nanny, is to pray that Christina will not be hurt."

Christina slept a little during the night from sheer exhaustion.

When she awoke and realised where she was, she got quickly to her feet.

Looking out of the window, she saw it was a dull day and the sky was cloudy.

She also thought it was very much hotter than it had been the day before.

She opened the window wide and found what breeze there was felt cooling on her face.

She was aware that she was thirsty.

If Terence Verley was determined to give her nothing, she would be longing for water before the day was past.

She looked down at the river, which seemed a long way beneath her.

She knew that it was impossible for her to escape from her prison, however hard she tried.

'There is . . . nothing I can . . . do,' she thought miserably, 'except go on praying, and hope that the Marquis — who by now should be awake — has . . . guessed what has . . . happened to me.'

There was no sign of Terence Verley coming up the steps to her.

She could hear someone moving about below and thought it must be Wills.

It was, in fact, nearly three hours later before heavy footsteps made her move back against the wall, as she felt in need of support.

"I came to see if you were still here," Terence Verley said in a thick voice.

He looked debauched.

Christina thought he must have drunk a great deal of wine last night and was now suffering from the after-effects.

"I . . . I am . . . all right," she said. "May I . . . have something to . . . to . . . drink?"

"No!" Terence replied. "Unless you want me to chuck you into the river!"

He glared at her before he added:

"That would certainly be throwing away a fortune!"

He looked her up and down in what she thought was an insulting manner before he added:

"Heaven knows if my Cousin will think you are worth so much money, but if he does not, at least I can prevent him from marrying you and doing me out of my title."

There was a snarl in his voice as he said the last word.

Christina knew that the mere idea of him not being the Marquis was enough to send him mad.

As if he had no wish to go on talking to her, he turned and went back down the steps.

He did not shut the door at the bottom of them as he had during the night.

She was therefore able to hear as he said to Wills:

"Is there a flag flying at the top of the mast?"

"Not th' one yer're lookin' fer," Wills answered, "but 'Is Lordship's standard ain't there either."

Listening, Christina knew that when a Marquis of Melverley was in residence, his standard was always flying from the rooftop.

She had reminded the Marquis of this.

He had therefore given orders that the standard should be flown, just as it had been in the old days.

She reasoned that if they had taken down the standard they were perhaps going to fly the white flag.

It was what Terence had asked for.

That would mean that the Marquis had given in to his blackmail and the money was being paid into his Bank in London.

'I cannot . . . bear him to . . . spend all that . . . on me,' Christina thought. 'It will mean that the repairs we talked about . . . cannot be . . . done, the Schools will not be opened, nor the Farms restocked.'

If Terence sent her back after the money had been paid, she would never be able to hold up her head again.

How could she, when so many people would suffer so that she was safe?

Then she thought that the Marquis, of all people, would be aware of this.

Somehow, in some magical way, he

would prevent his Cousin's wicked plot from being successful.

She went again to the window.

Now it seemed hotter than it had been when she had first woken.

Yet the sky was still overcast.

It occurred to her that there might be a thunderstorm.

If it rained, she would at least be able to catch some of the raindrops in her hands.

The hours passed slowly.

She heard the two men moving about below.

She guessed that Wills was preparing a Luncheon for his Master.

She supposed he must have brought it with him when he came back from looking to see if the white flag was flying.

She could hear sounds as if boxes or tins were being opened.

Then came the sound of a cork popping from a bottle.

A little while later the same sound came again.

She was sure Terence was drinking heavily.

Another hour passed.

Then she heard Terence order:

"Go and see if that damned flag is there!"

"Ai'll go wen Ai've packed these things up," Wills replied.

"Do as I tell you!" Terence roared. "I am fed up to the teeth with sitting about here. I want to get back to London."

"So do Ai," Wills agreed, "but us can't go back wi'out th' money."

"What the hell is he waiting for, I would like to know," Terence snarled. "If I thought he could hear that blasted girl's screams, I would beat her now to hurry him up."

He was obviously working himself into a rage, and Christina heard Wills say soothingly:

"Now, 'ave anovver drink, an' Ai'll go an look fer th' flag."

As he spoke, there came a clap of thunder which made Christina jump.

It had been so hot and overcast, she had thought there might be a thunderstorm.

The clap was followed by another, and then another.

It was obvious that the storm was coming nearer and was an extremely noisy one.

The next clap of thunder was practically overhead.

She shut her eyes so as not to see the lightning, and heard the rain begin to pour down.

Eagerly, because by now she was very thirsty, she held both her hands out of the window.

As the rain splashed into them, she drank what she could.

The water was cool and certainly relieved the dryness of her throat.

The lightning, however, dazzled her eyes, and the noise overhead was almost deafening.

She moved away from the window.

She sat down on the other side of the room on the rug on which she had slept.

The thunderstorm continued.

It seemed at one moment to fade away, then to return even more violently.

She could hear Terence shouting below.

The noise of the storm, however, made it impossible to hear what he was saying.

She thought he must be giving orders to Wills.

He was obviously being sensible enough

not to go out until the storm was over.

Christina shut her eyes.

Then she was praying again that the Marquis would somehow understand where she was.

She heard a sudden sound.

It did not seem to be connected with the storm, and she opened her eyes.

For a moment she thought she must be dreaming.

Through the open window there came a man's leg.

Before she could realise that it was real, it was followed by another.

She gave a cry that seemed to come from the very depths of her heart.

Then she jumped to her feet and ran towards the window.

It was the Marquis!

The Marquis himself was standing inside the room in which she was imprisoned!

She threw herself against him.

He put his arms around her, and pulled her close to him.

"Y-You . . . have come! You . . . h-have . . . come!" she managed to gasp.

Then his lips were on hers, and she knew she was not dreaming.

He was real.

Her prayers had been answered and he had found her.

He kissed her fiercely, possessively, then he raised his head.

"They have not hurt you?" he asked.

"N-No . . . no . . . I . . . I tried . . . to . . . t-tell you where I . . . was."

She could hardly say the words, and even as she spoke there was another sound from below.

This time it was that of a shot being fired from a pistol.

She gave a cry, and the Marquis tightened his hold of her.

"Do not be afraid," he said.

There was another shot, then two more.

Christina was trembling.

"Wh-what is . . . h-happening?" she whispered.

She saw that the Marquis had turned his head towards the stairs and was listening.

There was a clap of thunder, but now it came from further away.

It was followed by two or three more shots from below.

The Marquis put Christina to one side, but she clung to him.

"I must go and see what is happening," he said.

"Oh, no! No!" Christina cried. "Your Cousin might . . . shoot . . . you!"

The Marquis did not reply.

Then, when he would have made for the stairs, she clung to him, saying desperately:

"Let me go . . . they will not . . . kill me!"

The Marquis turned to look at her and smiled.

"Do you really think, my Darling, that I would let you do that for me?" he asked. "I am sure that Yates and the men I brought with me have managed without any help."

"I am . . . frightened . . . I am . . . frightened for . . . you!" Christina cried frantically. "He wants to . . . kill you . . . so that . . . he can be . . . the Marquis!"

"I know that," the Marquis answered, "and I promise you, that is something he will never be!"

By now he had reached the top of the steps.

"Just wait here until I come back," he said. "I will not be long, and I will not allow my disreputable Cousin to kill me."

"Y-you . . . cannot be . . . certain,"

Christina said desperately.

But it was too late.

The Marquis was running down the steps, and when he reached the bottom, he disappeared.

She stood where he had left her, aware that her heart was beating frantically.

She put her hand up to cover it.

She found that the front of her dressing-gown was wet.

It was only then that it dawned on her that the Marquis had swum the river before climbing up the side of the Mill to reach her.

He was all in black, and she knew it was because he would not be seen in the river.

All that mattered was, he had come!

The Marquis reached the bottom cautiously, just in case his Cousin took a shot at him.

He was certain that, if Terence should kill him, he would easily explain it away.

He had meant the bullet, of course, for the other people who were attacking him.

The first person the Marquis saw was

Yates, looking decidedly pleased with himself.

He was holding a pistol in his right hand.

The two other men whom the Marquis had brought with him to rescue Christina came from the village.

They had only recently returned home, having fought at the Battle of Waterloo and then been in the Army of Occupation.

It was Yates who had told him they were available.

He had brought them to the Hall.

The Marquis had seen the excitement in their eyes when he told them what he wished them to do.

They had carried out his instructions to the letter.

He had intended to wait until it was dark to rescue Christina.

When he realised there was going to be a thunderstorm, he thought this would give him even better cover.

It was unlikely, too, that Terence and Wills would be expecting him.

The two ex-soldiers had camouflaged themselves with the branches of trees and shrubs.

On the Marquis's instructions, they

had approached the old Mill, crawling over the flat ground.

He thought it likely that neither Terence nor Wills would be keeping watch in daylight.

They would therefore not see the two small "bushes" coming nearer and nearer.

Yates had followed behind them, and all three men were armed.

They advanced as near to the field as possible before they started to crawl.

The Marquis, going in another direction, had swum the river.

The torrential rain would, he knew, prevent him from being heard.

Once he reached the Mill he had found no difficulty in climbing up the dilapidated building.

The broken bricks made excellent footholds.

As he laughingly said to Christina afterwards:

"I did not find the old Mill half as difficult as the Pyrenees!"

Now, as he looked round the lower room of the Mill, the two ex-soldiers came in from outside.

They were pulling off their camouflage as they did so.

The Marquis looked at them question-ingly, and one man reported:

"Us did exactly as ye said, M'Lord."

"I am deeply grateful to you," the Marquis replied. "What has happened to the two men you were attacking?"

"Th' little man shot at us first," one of the men answered, "but 'e made a mess o' it, an' th' bullet passed right over me 'ead!"

"After that, us gives it to 'em!" the other man added. "Th' bigger man were shootin' wildly, wi'out takin' aim."

He spoke scornfully.

"What have you done with the bod-ies?" the Marquis asked.

"Chucked 'em in th' whirlpool, M'Lord," an ex-soldier answered, "them be dead as doornails, an' no-un' ain't ever come outa that pool."

He laughed as if he had made a joke before he added:

"There'll be no talk about it an' no-uns likely t' go down after 'em!"

There was a pause before the Marquis said quietly:

"I am extremely grateful to you both. I suggest now you go home and change your clothes. Come up to the Hall this evening, and I will give you what I hope you will think is ample reward for your services."

"It's bin a real pleasure, M'Lord," the other soldier replied, "an' jes' like ol' times t'be defeatin' a bad enemy!"

"Tha' be true," the other one agreed, "but them 'Frenchies' were better shots!"

The Marquis held up his hand and said:

"I want you to give me your word that you will not speak of this to anyone. Nothing must be said in the village, or in your homes."

"Ye can rely on us, M'Lord," one of the men replied. "Oi 'opes as ye'll remember us if there be any more difficulties like Yer Lordship's jes' 'ad."

"I will bear that in mind," the Marquis said quietly, "and I shall know who will help me."

He saw that was what they wanted to hear.

They pulled the last remaining bits of camouflage from their backs.

Then they set off, laughing happily, across the fields in the direction of the Hall.

The Marquis looked at Yates, who said:

"Ai ain't enjoyed meself so much since we were in France, M'Lord. That's the end o' Mr. Terence, an' good riddance!"

"I agree with you," the Marquis answered, "but it would be a great mistake for anyone else to know what has happened."

"Mum's th' word!" Yates said. "Yer can trust me, as yer well knows. Ai'll go now an' fetch th' carriage from where Ai 'id it b'ind them trees."

He pointed in the distance, and the Marquis said:

"Thank you, Yates, and hurry! As you can see, I am very wet."

"Ai puts a change o' clothes in the carriage, M'Lord," Yates replied, "an' Ai'll 'ave it 'ere afore yer can say 'Jack Robinson'!"

As Yates started to run off towards the trees, the Marquis sighed.

Then he turned towards the stairs.

Before he could start to climb them, Christina came hurrying down.

"Wh-what has . . . happened? Where has . . . everybody . . . gone?" she asked.

The Marquis put his arms around her.

"It is all over, my Darling," he said, "and I promise you — such a thing will never happen again."

"I was . . . listening," Christina said, "and I think I heard . . . someone say that your . . . Cousin Terence was . . . in the . . . whirlpool."

"You must forget what you heard and what has happened," the Marquis answered. "As I have already said, this will never happen again, and we do not want anyone to know or to talk about it."

"No. No . . . of course not," Christina agreed, and you are safe . . . you are . . . really safe!"

"Thanks to you," the Marquis said gently. "And now, my Precious, we can go back to Melverley and decide how quickly we can be married."

Christina stared at him.

"M-married?"

The Marquis smiled.

"I love you, my lovely one, and I think you love me."

He pulled her close to him, and she said:

"I . . . I love you . . . I love you . . . but I never thought that you would . . . love me. How can you . . . want to . . . m-marry me?"

"Very easily," the Marquis answered, "because when I thought I had lost you, I knew I had lost my most treasured possession."

As he finished speaking, his lips were on hers.

His kiss was urgent, possessive, and passionate.

Christina knew he was telling her without words how afraid he had been of losing her.

She felt as if the Heavens had opened and the Angels were singing.

How could it be possible that she was in the Marquis's arms and he was kissing her?

And yet he was!

"I love you . . . I love . . . you," she said again.

"And I adore you," the Marquis answered, and his voice was very deep. "You are mine, Christina, and I will never, never lose you!"

It seemed only a few minutes before Yates arrived back with the carriage.

He tied the horses to some railings so they could not move away.

He carried some dry clothes, and went with the Marquis to the room above to help him change.

It was not long before they came down again.

The Marquis was now looking as he always did, extremely smart and very handsome.

Christina said shyly:

187

"Now I feel . . . embarrassed . . . in only my . . . dressing-gown."

"You look adorable," the Marquis said firmly, "and I had no idea when I thought you were a ghost that your hair was so long."

She blushed and he said:

"Could anyone look more like the Princess in a fairy-tale?"

She looked shy, and he added:

"Perhaps I am the Black Knight who rescues you from the Dragon."

"Not the Black Knight," Christina protested, "but St. Christopher himself! You swam across . . . the river to . . . rescue me! And I still . . . cannot believe that you . . . climbed up the Mill to . . . reach me!"

The Marquis laughed and helped her into the carriage, which was closed as he sat down beside her.

Yates, who was driving, started the horses and, as they moved off, the Marquis said:

"How can you have been so ingenious in the way you told me where you were?"

"D-did you . . . know as . . . soon as you . . . read my m-message that I was . . . imprisoned in the . . . old Mill?"

The Marquis's eyes twinkled.

"I cannot take all the credit for that," he said. "It was in fact Miss Dickson and your Nanny who knew where you were when you said you were 'praying to St. Christopher.' "

"And he . . . did save me," Christina whispered. "I prayed very . . . hard that he would . . . tell you where I . . . was."

The Marquis pulled her into his arms.

"I do not want to think how frightened I was that my mad Cousin Terence would harm you, my Darling."

"And you are . . . really sure that . . . you love me?" Christina asked.

"So sure that I not only love you, but cannot live without you," the Marquis answered. "We have so much to do, my Darling, that the sooner we are married and start working together, the happier we can make all those who depend upon us."

Christina put up her hand to touch his face very tenderly.

"I . . . I find it . . . difficult to believe that you are . . . real," she said. "Are you certain that . . . if you m-marry me you will not . . . be bored and . . . want to go back . . . to London and be with the . . . beautiful Ladies there instead of . . . staying at Melverley?"

The Marquis knew the question was very important and said quietly:

"Of course, my Precious, there have been 'Beautiful Ladies,' as you call them, in my life, but I now know that until this moment I was never truly in love. It was when I thought I had lost you that I knew there was something different between us, something I have never felt before for any other woman."

"Wh-what . . . is it?" Christina whispered.

"It is that my heart beats in tune with your heart," the Marquis said, and smiled. "My soul speaks to your soul and I respond to you, my Precious, in a way I have never done before with any other woman."

Christina gave a little cry.

"Oh . . . is that true . . . really true?"

"You know I would not lie to you," the Marquis said. "It is true, my lovely little Fairy Princess, because you are the other part of me and I am the other part of you, and we will love each other for ever."

"That is . . . how I have . . . always wanted to be loved," Christina was trying to say.

But it was impossible to speak because the Marquis was kissing her again.

Once more the Angels were singing and the Heaven which God has created especially for lovers was waiting for them.

ABOUT THE AUTHOR

Barbara Cartland, the world's most famous romantic novelist, who is also an historian, playwright, lecturer, political speaker and television personality, has now written over 605 books and sold over six hundred and twenty million copies all over the world.

She has also had many historical works published and has written four autobiographies as well as the biographies of her mother and that of her brother, Ronald Cartland, who was the first Member of Parliament to be killed in the last war. This book has a preface by Sir Winston Churchill and has just been republished with an introduction by Sir Arthur Bryant.

Love at the Helm, a novel written with the help and inspiration of the late Earl Mountbatten of Burma, Great Uncle of His Royal Highness, The Prince of Wales, is being sold for the Mountbatten Memorial Trust.

She has broken the world record for the last twenty years by writing an average of twenty-three books a year. In the *Guinness Book of World Records* she is listed as the world's top-selling author.

Miss Cartland in 1987 sang an Album of Love Songs with the Royal Philharmonic Orchestra.

In private life Barbara Cartland, who is a Dame of the Order of St. John of Jerusalem and Chairman of the St. John Council in Hertfordshire, has fought for better conditions and salaries for Midwives and Nurses.

She championed the cause for the Elderly in 1956, invoking a Government Enquiry into the "Housing Conditions of Old People."

In 1962 she had the Law of England changed so that Local Authorities had to provide camps for their own Gypsies. This has meant that since then thousands and thousands of Gypsy children have been able to go to School, which they had never been able to do in the past, as their caravans were moved every twenty-four hours by the Police.

There are now fifteen camps in Hertfordshire and Barbara Cartland has her own Romany Gypsy Camp called "Barbaraville" by the Gypsies.

Her designs "Decorating with Love" are being sold all over the U.S.A. and the National Home Fashions League made her, in 1981, "Woman of Achievement."

She is unique in that she was one and two in the Dalton list of Best Sellers, and one week had four books in the top twenty.

Barbara Cartland's book *Getting Older, Growing Younger* has been published in Great Britain and the U.S.A. and her fifth cookery book, *The Romance of Food*, is now being used by the House of Commons.

In 1984 she received at Kennedy Airport America's Bishop Wright Air Industry Award for her contribution to the development of aviation. In 1931 she and two R.A.F. Officers thought of, and carried, the first aeroplane-towed glider airmail.

During the War she was Chief Lady Welfare Officer in Bedfordshire, looking after 20,000 Servicemen and women. She thought of having a pool of Wedding Dresses at the War Office so a Service Bride could hire a gown for the day.

She bought 1,000 gowns without coupons for the A.T.S., the W.A.A.F's and the W.R.E.N.S. In 1945 Barbara Cartland received the Certificate of Merit from Eastern Command.

In 1964 Barbara Cartland founded the National Association for Health of which she is the President, as a front for all the Health Stores and for any product made as alternative medicine.

This is now a £65 million turnover a year, with one-third going in export.

In January 1968 she received *La Médeille de Vermeil de la Ville de Paris.* This is the highest award to be given in France by the City of Paris. She has sold 30 million books in France.

In March 1988 Barbara Cartland was asked by the Indian Government to open their Health Resort outside Delhi. This is almost the largest Health Resort in the world.

Barbara Cartland was received with great enthusiasm by her fans, who feted her at a reception in the City, and she received the gift of an embossed plate from the Government.

Barbara Cartland was made a Dame of the Order of the British Empire in the 1991 New Year's Honours List by Her Majesty, The Queen, for her contribution to Literature and also for her years of work for the community.

Dame Barbara has now written 605 books, the greatest number by a British author, passing the 564 books written by John Creasey.